STANDING ON HER BUSINESS 2

REAL AS IT GETS

DG SANTANA

LOCK DOWN PUBLICATIONS AND CA$H PRESENTS

Lock Down Publications

P.O. Box 944

Stockbridge, GA 30281

www.lockdownpublications.com

Like our page on Facebook: Lock Down Publications

www.facebook.com/lockdownpublications.ldp

STAY CONNECTED WITH US!

Text **LOCKDOWN** to 22828 to stay up-to-date with new releases, sneak peaks, contests and more...

Like our page on Facebook:
Lock Down Publications

Join Lock Down Publications/The New Era Reading Group

Visit our website:
www.lockdownpublications.com

Follow us on Instagram:
Lock Down Publications

Email Us: We want to hear from you!

CHAPTER 1
LANEY

LANEY WOKE UP AND THOUGHT SHE WAS DREAMING WHEN she felt Zion's strong grip around her waist. The pressure and warmth from his body plastered up against her backside felt like Heaven. She'd fantasized about mornings like this for so long, and now that it was a reality, it would take some time to get used to.

They had slept on top of three blankets laid out on the floor because Zion couldn't sleep in the bed. It was too comfortable for him after sleeping on a hard prison mattress for so long. Their soft mattress felt weird to him. He would get out of the bed in the middle of the night and make a pallet on the floor, and every time, she'd wake up and join him on the floor. She didn't care where they were sleeping as long as she was sleeping with her man. She would've drove to the prison and slept with him on one of those mattresses if they would've let her.

She sat up, lit a half-smoked joint from the night before, and just stared at him for a moment. She was so grateful to have him there by her side in the flesh. It was just a month ago when she had watched Zion fight for his life in that tournament. She was sure that it would be her last time seeing him, but he triumphed against the odds, and it had to be God. She would've been crushed if he wouldn't have made it out.

"Bae! Wake up, you got training this morning!" she informed before raining kisses all over his face.

He crumbled his face up, acting like her affection annoyed him, but she knew he couldn't get enough of her ass, and it was definitely vice versa.

"Damn, I swear I don't feel like getting up, man," he informed after a long, prolonged stretch.

He had to get up though because Yuteg kept his word and did what he said he would do if Zion made it out of that tournament. He plugged Zion in with a professional management team that was setting up his debut commercial boxing match. He was about to take the boxing world by storm.

He got up and made his way to their bathroom in nothing but a pair of grey boxer briefs. Laney bit her lip as she watched him walk away, looking at his tattoo covered backside. "Matter of fact, I'm going to go ahead and get in there with you. I got shit to do my damn self."

She got up, wearing nothing but a lingerie set and a mischievous smile. Her man was home, and she was feeling whole. He was the only man she allowed herself to be soft and prissy with.

They got into the hot shower together, and their bodies instantly clicked like two huge magnets. They held one another and shared a long, passionate kiss. Laney had speakers installed in her bathroom, and Marian Carey's *We Belong Together* remix played smoothly. She couldn't explain the feeling, but the feeling was euphoric.

After a small while, he bent down a little more and picked her up off of her feet. She knew what time it was, so she reached down and grabbed his dick, so she could guide it inside of her. She didn't think she'd ever grow tired of feeling him inside of her. The dick hit different when you were in love with the nigga it was attached to. There was literally no better feeling to a woman.

She wrapped both hands around his neck and clasped her hands together as he began to bounce her up and down on his hard dick that was curved inward. He was hitting all the right spots, and she couldn't help but bite her lip and roll her eyes to the back of her head.

"Uhmmm! I want you inside of me foreva, nigga! I love how you beat this pussy up!" She spoke into his ear while hugging him close.

He didn't respond verbally, just gripped her ass tighter and began fucking her harder, causing her juices to flow. She began to squirt on his dick, but since they were in the shower, he probably didn't even notice. He continued to pump away until he released himself inside of her, then he gently placed her down, so they could wash properly.

Zion was running late for his training session, so she washed him first, so he could hurry out the shower, but she stayed in there long after him. She washed herself slowly while deep in her own thoughts. She couldn't thank God enough her uniting her with the love of her life. Just as she predicted, shit was better with him actually being there. Of course, shit wasn't perfect, but definitely better. He supported her, and she supported him. She couldn't ask for too much more than that at the moment.

Her mind began to shift from the love of her life to her business life. She had come a *long* way since she'd taken over Rock Nation, but she still had a long way to go, and giving up wasn't an option, so she had to see it through. Murk and Tory had become her crutches, and she was very grateful for them, but it wasn't enough. Rock Nation was growing each day, and it came with more problems.

They were problems she eventually had to oversee, so she was challenged with the task of restructuring the chain of command, so there'd be less weight on her shoulders.

CHAPTER 2
MURK

MURK SAT IN HIS DAUGHTER'S ROOM, WATCHING AN animated movie with her. She was literally the only good thing in his life, and he felt like he didn't deserve her in so many ways. She was growing before his eyes, and it steadily amazed him. She was turning seven soon, and it seemed like she had the smarts of a teenager already. She obviously got her brains from him because her mother was slower than a tax return, but at least she had her mother's thick, curly hair. It was cute on her.

"Daddy, you going to take me to Disney World this summer? I asked Mama, and she told me to talk to you," she said while looking up at him with those sharp, slanted, grey eyes she inherited from him.

He smiled, showing his slightly crooked, but white, teeth. "Of course she said that, but yeah, I'll take you. Just remind me beforehand," he assured her before looking down at his vibrating phone. It was Swiss.

He kissed her on the forehead and stepped out of her

room into the hallway to take the call. "Yo. This better be good. You interrupting daddy daughter time, fool."

"You need to get your ass over there and check on Glock before he do something stupid," Swiss strongly suggested.

Murk sighed heavily. "What now, man?"

"His little sister got killed this morning by two white police cops. She was in a stolen car with her boyfriend, and they got pulled over. I don't need to tell you how the rest went down. Long story short, his little sister got caught up in the middle of it. Now she laid up in the morgue."

"Fuck!" Murk spat before hanging up on Swiss and attempting to call Glock. It went straight to voicemail twice. He tried calling his other phone and got the same result.

Murk pocketed his phone and went back into Aria's room to let her know that he had to go and that he loved her before storming out of the house.

"Where you going? We was supposed to take her skating tonight," his baby mother, Anaria, reminded from the couch in the living room.

"We going to have to take her another time. Got some shit going on right now," he informed urgently.

She sucked her teeth. "It's always some shit going on, nigga. You going to end up breaking that girl's heart like you did mines."

"Man, I don't got time for all this shit right now. I'll talk to you later," he spat before disappearing out of the house.

Murk hopped in his Jaguar and zipped through traffic, on his way to Glock City. Whenever Glock wasn't out on a mission, he was at the headquarters. He never went anywhere else unless it meant business, so Murk knew exactly where to find him.

He told Swiss to grab a few Vultures and meet him at the entrance of the apartment complex, and like clockwork, they were there, parked inside of a black Yukon waiting on him as he arrived.

"What it's looking like?" Murk asked Swiss after pulling up next to the Yukon and rolling down his windows.

Swiss nodded toward the apartment buildings. "I think he's in there. I talked to one of dem lil' bitches, and she said she ain't seen no group of niggas leave lately, so he got to be still here. If he do make a move, it won't be until after dark."

"That's what we here to prevent," Murk informed before pressing the gas pedal and zipping past the entry gates into Glock City.

They drove back to Glock's building and hopped out. The park was full of young killers as usual, but today, the energy was different. Everybody had grimaces and mugs on their faces. They obviously all knew Glock's little sister, and her death was felt by them all.

A familiar face approached Murk as he made his way past them toward the building. It was Glock's lieutenant, Ruga. He was a short, black, ugly muthafucka, but in his mind, he was 6'6". "This ain't the time right now, big bruh. I been knowing Glock my whole life, and I ain't never seen him like this. You might want to double back another time."

Murk locked eyes with the youngin and nodded his

understanding. "I can only imagine what he feeling right now, but I got to go up there and talk to him. I can't let him crash out. I got plans for the lil' nigga."

Ruga took a deep breath and looked to be weighing his options. "He told me to make sure he don't get bothered, but I think he'll understand if I let you up there, but Swiss and them got to stay out here with us."

Murk nodded his agreement before making his way into the apartment building. He got on the elevator and took it up to the fifth floor where Glock's apartment was. He knocked on Glock's door and inwardly prepared himself to deal with the young nigga.

To his surprise, Glock answered the door with a dry face. He hadn't been crying and seemed unfazed. The average person would've missed it, but Murk could see the pain and hurt all in his eyes. It was all there, and Murk instantly felt his protégé's pain. "I'm sorry that shit happened, lil' bruh. I swear I am."

"I'm not trying to hear that shit, Murk. Them crackers killed my baby fucking sister, man. My baby sister, bruh! They going to die tonight, and it's not nothing you, Tory, Laney, or J-Rock can do about it. I'm going to kill they families and make them watch before I kill them," he promised sternly, but he had a cold calmness in his voice that Murk knew all too well.

Murk sighed heavily. "Then what? You know that's a suicide mission, right?"

Glock stood in the doorway, staring at him with a straight face. It was obvious that he didn't give a fuck.

"Use your head, young nigga. You going to throw it all

away just like that? It's other smarter ways we can handle this."

Glock took a step back and slammed the door in Murk's face. Murk was caught off guard by that one. Glock would get a pass for the disrespect due to the nature of the situation, but he couldn't let the lil' nigga follow through with his plan of retaliation because he wouldn't get a pass for that, and he had big plans for Glock.

CHAPTER 3

LANEY

AFTER GETTING DRESSED, LANEY MADE HERSELF A QUICK breakfast and headed out. She drove herself to Static Lounge and made her way to her office. Although she didn't manage the place anymore, she still used it as her base of operations. It would always be her second home.

"Craig, if you don't get your feet off of my desk, I'm going to stab you," she promised half-jokingly. "You have your own office downstairs. Why do you insist on being in mines?"

After realizing Craig's gift of finesse and his way around people, Laney appointed him manager over the lounge. He was doing a better job than she expected, like he was meant for the shit. It was a relief for her because it was one less thing she had to worry about on her plate.

"Man, I can't get that new paint smell out of my shit. I can't stand it. So, until it goes away, I'll be working out of your shit," he informed unapologetically.

"Get your ass up out of my chair and hit that sofa. Hell wrong with you?" she commanded, making a show of attempting to knock him across the head with her Louis bag.

He got up with a smirk and relocated to the sofa.

"How's things going in here though? Still running a tight ship?" she asked with a raised brow.

"You damn right!" he assured. "Beyoncé just made a reservation for a brunch with her mother next week. I convinced her assistant to convince her to make a photo-shoot out of the whole thing. So, that'll be real good for business."

"Wowww! Good job, Craig," she said with actual applause. "I knew I did the right thing by giving you this job."

There was an urgent knock on her office door, and one of the waitresses stuck her head in. "Murk is on his way up here. I told him to wait but..."

"Shut the fuck up!" Murk spat as he appeared in the doorway. He shoved the waitress out of the way like a ragdoll and closed the door in her face after stepping into the office. "Bitch seen security let me in, and she still run up here like I'm a threat."

"She did right. That's how I trained her," Laney stated matter-of-factly. "And don't put your hands on none of my employees again, nigga! Hell wrong wit you? What the hell you want anyway?" Her tone was stern, but the curiousness in her voice was stronger.

Murk looked down at Craig. "Beat it, nigga. This above yo' pay grade."

"Check it out, son... I don't care how many so-called bodies you dropped. You going to talk to me with some fuckin' respect. You hear me?" Craig spat after popping up off the couch like a grasshopper.

Laney sighed as she sat there and watched them stand off as if they were about to throw down right there in the middle of her office. She was impressed by Craig's fearlessness and the way he looked up at Murk without a hint of fear, but she didn't have time for this shit. "Go make your rounds, Craig. Let me holler at Murk."

Craig released a clenched sigh of his own before leaving the office reluctantly.

"Sit your rude ass down, nigga! All these years and you still ain't grow no damn people skills? Out here acting like you still nineteen and shit. Grow the fuck up!"

Murk waved her off as he began to pace the floor back-and-forth. "Fuck all that. We got a *big* fucking problem!"

"That's obvious, judging by your presence. What is it?"

"You heard about that young boy and girl that got killed in a traffic stop last night?" he asked.

She nodded. "Yeah, seen somebody post about it on Facebook earlier this morning. How is that a problem for us though?"

"The girl that got killed was Glock's little sister, and they was tight as hell. He basically raised her," he informed seriously. "That lil' nigga want blood, and I looked him in his eyes. He dead ass serious. Talking about killing the families of the officers and shit."

Laney's face crumbled. "What the fuck?! Is he stupid? I understand he grieving, but I can't allow him to bring that type of heat down on the nation. You got to talk some sense into him."

"Nahhh." Murk shook his head rapidly. "I'm telling you ain't no stopping the lil' nigga. I'll have to kill him... I can talk him out of fucking with the families, but the only option I see is helping him snatch the officers up. That's the lesser evil, and it'll be less heat if I get involved."

"You must be smoking crack, nigga! Hell no! I'm not having it. You better go stop that lil' nigga," she commanded.

"You not listening, Laney... I'm going to have to wipe out the whole Glock Gang, and I'm not about to do that. I'm not about to let that nigga go fuck with them folks' families either, so just let me step in and make sure the shit get done right. Think about it. Two missing officers is wayyyy better than two officers massacred in their homes along with their families."

Laney released another sigh and sat back in her seat, assessing the situation at hand. It was a tough call, and she had an impossible decision to make. That seemed like the story of her damn life lately.

Someone else knocked on the door. "Come back!" Laney yelled, but the door opened anyway. She was about to curse whoever it was out until she noticed it was Tory walking in.

"What the hell you want, Tory? This better not be about the Virginia thing. I told you to leave that alone. I'm not in the mood," she warned seriously.

Tory shook his head while unbuttoning his blue jean jacket. "Nahhh, this some whole other business right here."

"I need the green light before I leave. This shit is serious, 'Ney!" Murk stated urgently.

Laney buried her face in her palms for a few moments and suddenly popped her head back up. "Go ahead, man, but make sure that shit is spotless. Turn them crackers into ghost. After Glock gets finished with them, make sure them bodies is *neverrrr* found."

"I got you," Murk assured before storming out of the office like a man on a mission.

"Do I even want to know?" Tory asked with a raised brow.

Laney shook her head. "No, but I want to know what the hell you want."

"It's not me this time," he assured with a smug shrug. "DG Donny's trying to holler at you."

"You talking about the nigga Manny's always rapping about? Ain't he locked up?" she asked in confusion.

Tory nodded. "Yeah, but apparently, he's still running his city from behind bars."

"What does he want though?" she asked curiously.

Tory shrugged again. "Shit, I don't know. That nigga won't budge. He insist on talking to your ass."

"Get him on the line," she instructed before burying her face back into her palms.

Tory took a seat across from her desk and dialed the number Donny gave him to reach him. He picked up on the third ring, and Tory passed the phone to her.

"Is this the head bitch in charge?" Donny asked with his notorious smugness. It was one of the things he was known for.

"The name is Laney, but yes, I am in charge... How can

I help you, sir?" she asked evenly, trying to maintain her professionalism.

Donny laughed. "Not sir! Just call me Donny, baby... but I do have a matter I need to discuss with you."

"I'm listening," Laney said while suppressing a sigh. She wasn't in the mood to deal with Donny, but he was a made man in Carolina, and she was curious about what he wanted.

"I had a talk with J-Rock before he disappeared, and we came to a clear agreement that Fayetteville is *off limits* for Rock Nation, so I'm trying to figure out why in the fuck do I hear whispers about your people doing business in my fucking city!" Donny's voice hardened. "Y'all may have North Carolina on lock, but don't forget that the DG empire extends all over the country. And everybody loves me. Y'all don't want a fucking war. I'll humble y'all asses real quick on some *300 Spartan* shit!"

Laney pulled the phone away from her ear and looked at it with a mug. "Listen, I never sanctioned anything out in Fayetteville. If any of mines is doing business around that way, they're being sneaky and will be dealt with. I'll have my general do an investigation and get to the bottom of it," she promised.

"I suggest you make that top priority," Donny strongly suggested before abruptly ending the call.

Laney slid the burner phone across the table. "You supposed to be on top of shit like this. Find out who's doing business in Fayetteville and bring them to me."

Tory nodded and left. He looked like he had something else to bother her with, but she clearly wasn't in the mood, so he just left the office. Laney released another sigh as he closed the door behind himself. She just shook her head as she contemplated on all of the current problems on her plate. She couldn't help the feeling of discouragement because she knew shit would get a whole lot worse before it got better.

CHAPTER 4

GLOCK

LATER ON THAT EVENING IN GLOCK CITY, GLOCK STOOD ON top of the gymnasium, looking down at most of his comrades. They were loyal young niggas, and most of them would follow him to the ends of the earth. He'd earned each of their respect, and they'd earned his, which was why he stood there explaining himself and the entire situation at hand.

"Listen... Everybody standing right here knows what Ja'Kiya meant to me. That was more than my little sister. She was like a fucking daughter to me. I raised her lil' ass and literally taught her everything she knew. She was a gutter bitch, but she was meant for way more than that. She was about to graduate high school early and go to college to be a fucking lawyer! A lawyer from these parts. Can y'all believe that? She wanted to be a criminal defense lawyer and start her own firm, just to help the fucking gang, man." He could tell that the pain in his voice swept over each of them.

Nobody responded. The park was quiet. All that could be heard was the cold wind breezing past and the nearby train on the tracks. "Well, none of that's going to get to happen now because those pussy ass crackers took her life. They took her chance to grow into a better woman and help her people. Now, I'm going to take something from they asses! If you going to walk away, you need to do it now. Nothing won't happen to you, and I'll understand. I'm not forcing nobody to go on this mission with me."

Two black Yukons approached as he ended his statement, and Glock clenched his teeth. *This nigga here don't get the fucking picture. He can't stop this shit,* Glock thought to himself as he made his way down from the gymnasium.

"You think they going to get in our way?" Ruga asked as he walked up and stood beside Glock.

Glock shrugged. "Ain't no telling. Let's go see."

Glock and Ruga approached the Yukons that were now parked. Vultures spilled out, holding their semi-automatic rifles. Glock didn't feel threatened though because that was just how they rocked. Black attire and big guns were a part of their dress code.

"I told you that you not going to be able to stop this shit, Murk. I'm going to take all the heat. This is a Glock Gang problem. It won't blow back on the nation," he promised after walking up on Murk.

Murk hung hallway out of the backseat of the truck with his door open. He sat with his elbows on his knees, looking hard at Glock. "That's what I'm here for. It ain't got to be no heat if you do it the smart way. Let us help y'all."

"Nahhhh, you going to try to spare them crackers, and I need that blood. Like tonight. Fuck all that waiting shit," Glock spat in a nonnegotiable manner.

Murk took the hoodie from off of his head and shook his head from side to side slowly. "Nobody's telling you to wait. We can get blood tonight. I already talked to Laney and got her to green light this shit. It's only two conditions though."

Glock lifted a brow. He was shocked that Murk convinced Laney to green light the retaliation, and he was curious about the conditions she'd set. "What conditions?"

"For one, you got to leave the families out of the equation, and secondly, we got to kidnap the crackers and make them disappear. Can't make a messy example out of them like you was planning to. Two missing officers will bring less heat than two officers executed along with their families," Murk reasoned carefully, obviously trying to get his point across to Glock.

Glock drew in a deep breath and ran his hand through his silky box braids that dangled freely. "Alright, man. I guess I can live with that... I appreciate you for getting Laney to green light this shit though. At least my head won't be on the chopping block."

Murk hopped down onto the concrete and closed the distance between them. He reached out his hand for an embrace. "I meant it when I said I fuck with you, lil' nigga. Ain't too many niggas built like us. Got to protect our kind at all costs."

CHAPTER 5
BIG BODY

BIG BODY WAS HITTING WEIGHTS AT THE INSIDE GYM HE had in his house on the westside. He could've afforded a better house in a better neighborhood, but he was smart enough not to purchase one. In the eyes of the government, he was broke, and he didn't want to give them a reason to be all up in his mix, so he lived below his means. The nigga still accepted food stamps and social security.

He had an average looking house, but he had it tricked out on the inside to make himself feel a little better about slumming it. He finished the last set of reps on the weight bench and took a Gatorade break. He was trying to turn his chubbiness into muscle. Ever since Zion came home, he was on Big Body and Tory's ass about their physical health and didn't give them a choice. Prison made that nigga aggressive as hell, way more aggressive than they remembered.

His contemplation was broken by the sound of someone ringing his doorbell. Every time someone rang his doorbell,

Yo Gotti's *Touchdown* played through the speakers in the house. He got up, grabbed his workout towel, and made his way to the front door.

It was his sergeant, Nitro. He stood on the other side of the door with a wide smile on his sneaky face. "You ain't going to believe this shit, big dawg."

Big Body squinted his eyes curiously. "By the look of that ugly ass smile on your face, I take it it's something good."

"Good ain't the word. We just hit for the fucking motherload!"

"So, why you ain't got it with you? Supposed to have some duffle bags in your hand or something. I told you to bring the shit directly to me," Big Body spat suspiciously.

Nitro laughed in his face. "Duffle bags? Nigga, I had to carry that shit out in trash bags. Follow me."

Big Body followed him over to the white van Nitro had parked in his driveway. Nitro opened the doors to the back of the van, and Big Body's mouth dropped. He was speechless. There were seven bulky trash bags in the back of the van, filled to the rim. It was the motherload indeed.

"So, all of this is money?" Big Body asked after pulling a bundle of fresh twenties out of the nearest bag.

Nitro nodded his head slowly. The wide smile never once left his face. Big Body had never seen him smile that hard as long as he'd known the young nigga. "Yup. All twenties as far as I could see."

"That's about three or four million cash. It has to be counterfeit. He wouldn't have just had this money sitting in his basement like this if it was authentic."

Nitro's smile vanished. "Nahhh, nahh. Look at that shit. That's real deal cash money right there."

"I been knowing Ice for years, and I been watching the nigga. Keeping real tabs on him. I know for a fact he got a plug on counterfeit cash, and I know for a fact he wouldn't even have this much money in cash anyway. Them niggas got overseas accounts and cryptocurrency and shit. This got to be fake money, but the upside to it is that this is some good ass counterfeit money. He probably paid a million real dollars for this shit, so we still hit his ass good."

Big Body waged an undercover war on Ice, and he planned on making the nigga suffer until he tapped out. He wouldn't stop until he ran Ice up out of the city. He fucked up when he pushed the issue to have those two BBG niggas killed. Big Body played it cool to Laney, but he couldn't — and wouldn't —let that go.

Nitro's smile was back. "So, how you want to flip this shit?"

"That's not your concern... I'm going to pay you a hundred thousand for getting the business handled, and you won't speak another word of this shit."

Nitro's smile was gone again. "A hundred thousand! Come on, big dawg. I know you not about to lil' boy me like that!"

"Yeah, nigga! A hundred thousand! You was just plotting on robbing a check cashing spot for thirty thousand before I put you on this lick, so you can pay all your bills. You better take that shit and run with it... Plus, don't think I forgot about the last mission you put together that got two of the lil homies jammed up. Your ass was supposed to get violated for that. Don't play with me, Nitro," he spat warningly.

He studied Nitro as he pouted inwardly. Tory was right. He wasn't to be trusted, but he was very useful, which was why Big Body kept him close.

"Alright, man. It's going to be 100 Gs in real money, right?" he asked hopefully.

"Yeah, nigga. All hundreds... Now, take these bags in my house and beat it. I'll have your money ready for you in a few days," he instructed before walking back into the house.

CHAPTER 6
MURK

LATER ON THAT NIGHT, ON THE EASTSIDE OF TOWN, MURK stood quietly in the corner of a basement. He studied Glock as he paced the floor in front of the two officers that robbed his baby sister for her precious life.

Murk kept his word and assisted Glock in snatching up the officers. It wasn't as hard as one would've thought. They caught both officers coming out of a bar together. Shit was like snatching up a few kids. Murk had them brought to one of his various workshop houses that he used strictly for situations such as this.

Two of the houses still held hostages from months ago for different purposes. It was just another day for Murk. Business as usual. It was what he did. He specialized in pain and suffering.

"Alright... I planned on killing y'all families in front of y'all and making y'all watch as a form of torture before killing y'all next... But y'all got my boss to thank for sparing the lives of y'all families. Now, I'm just trying to come up with the best way to kill y'all crackers in my head," Glock stated casually without breaking his pace.

The officers were both tied up on the basement floor, looking up at him with wide eyes. Murk could tell that they had sobered up by now, and their fucked-up reality was hitting them. They probably couldn't believe they were about to be held accountable for their actions.

"What you think, Murk?" Glock asked as he glanced toward the corner.

Murk shrugged. "This your show, lil' nigga, and that was your sister's life that they took... I don't care how you kill them. I'm just here to make sure they disappear afterward and never get found."

"Shut the fuck up!" Glock roared as he came down with a hard Timberland boot to one of their faces. His mumbles couldn't be made out through the mouth gag, but Glock obviously wasn't trying to hear it. "Need to be praying to Hitler because that's who y'all racist asses is going to meet!" Glock spat before kicking the other one in the face.

He walked over to the long torture table that Murk had set up for him. A wide variety of potential torture tools were laid out neatly on the table. Glock scanned the table carefully for a moment before picking up a wooden bat.

"Gonna keep it simple, huh? I like that. Good choice," Murk encouraged as he folded his arms and put one foot up on the wall like he was about to watch a basketball game in a park.

Glock didn't respond. He just walked back over to the officers and let it rip. The young nigga had some good stamina because he literally beat them for about ten minutes straight. And anyone who'd gotten active knew that that was a long fucking time to be swinging a bat nonstop. By the time Glock was done with them, they were unrecognizable and covered in their own blood. There was no doubt that just about every bone in their bodies were broken badly.

Glock dropped the bat and plopped down on the floor. He raised his knees up to his chest, wrapped his arms around his knees, and buried his face into the space in between. Murk felt for his young nigga. He knew exactly how Glock was feeling. He could've killed those officers a million times over, and it still wouldn't bring his sister back. She was gone *forever*.

Murk didn't say a word, just sent a text to Swiss, telling him to send in a few of the Vultures to do their part.

CHAPTER 7
LANEY

MEANWHILE, AT LANEY'S SPOT, SHE ENJOYED A refreshing candlelit dinner with her man. Her and Zion had made it home around the same time and decided to do a big dinner for themselves. She cooked, and he helped. The lamb chops and shrimp came out perfectly, and they both cleared their plates.

"You worked up an appetite at that gym, I see." She pointed out to Zion, who had about triple the amount of food on his plates.

Zion displayed his signature sexy smirk. "Fucking right... My trainer trying to put me on this strict diet but fuck all that. I told that nigga I'm going to eat whatever I want."

"Now, baby, you know you got to listen to your trainer," she advised.

"Not when he's wrong. I already gave up pork. Shit, that's enough compromise. I told that nigga as long as I'm not falling behind on training, I don't want to hear shit," he recited with finality.

His stern dominance turned her on to the max. He was so mannish and was a perfect fit for her. She was a boss bitch with command over a thousand men and hundreds of women. It took a certain type of man to tame a woman like her, and Zion was that type of man. She had absolutely no problem submitting to his ass, and she didn't think she ever would.

"I feel you, baby. Well, either way, I'm here to support you. Diet or no diet, I know you're going to do your thing in that ring when it comes time."

"I promise you them niggas got another thing coming. I'm going to make them feel my pain, literally... Anyway, how was your day?"

Laney did a mental recap of her day and was about to leave the part about the police officers out, but she made Zion a promise to tell him everything, so that was what she did. She told him about the unexpected call she received from DG Donny and Glock's situation.

"Damn, what the fuck?! So, you really green lighted that shit, bae? Shit got me worried now. I know the police going to want some get back, and I don't need this shit blowing back on you," he said, not trying to hide the concern in his voice.

Laney shook her head. "Nah, that's why I got involved to make sure that shit doesn't fall back on the nation. Glock originally wanted to make both officers watch their families being killed before doing them. Now, two massacres like that would've had shit way hotter than just two missing officers. Their bodies will never be found, so the authorities can't do shit but speculate. They won't be able to come after us officially... Plus, it'll be a good lesson to the other trigger-happy crackers holding a badge out there."

"Damnnn," he responded, just staring at her from across the table. "You a whole queenpin out here. I can't get over that shit." He chuckled through the last sentence.

The look he gave her was one of admiration. He didn't have a hint of disappointment in his eyes or his voice. That was why she loved him. He never once judged her about anything. "Long as you sticking beside me, I'm going to be just fine. Don't turn your back on a bitch when you make it big boxing now."

He shot her a straight face. "Now you know better than that. I'll quit this boxing shit right now and help you run the nation if that's what you need," he assured seriously.

"Now you know I would never. We going to make it work, baby. Between our two worlds, we going to meet dead in the middle."

She knew things would get difficult once he became mainstream, but that was a bridge they'd have to cross once they got there. For now, she was enjoying her man and having him by her side.

———

After dinner, they cleaned up after themselves and caught a movie. About halfway through the movie, Laney received a call. It was Karmen's crazy ass.

"Heyyyy, Mama!" Laney greeted excitedly after answering the call.

The two had formed an even deeper bond over the months. Karmen had admitted how she felt like Laney was the daughter she'd always wanted, and Laney admitted that she was the only real mother figure she ever had in her life. After that, the two adopted each other and began to treat each other like mother and daughter.

"My beautiful baby girl, how are you this evening?" asked Karmen.

Laney looked over at Zion, who was already looking at her. "I'm good. Just at the spot, watching a movie with my husband."

"Good. It's about time I met him anyway," said Karmen. "I'm about to text you an address. Meet me there."

"Now?" Laney asked with a curious expression.

"Yes, now, girl. It's important."

Laney rolled her eyes. "It's always important let you tell it."

"Don't make me have to come get you, little girl. You know I will... Make sure you bring Zion," Karmen threatened jokingly.

"Okayyyuhh! I'll be there soon," she assured before ending the call. Zion was still staring at her when she hung up the phone. "Whattt?"

"That was Karmen, right? What she want?" he asked curiously. He knew all about Karmen, and Karmen knew all about him, but they'd never met.

Laney nodded her head up and down. "Yeah, and she wants to meet you."

"I guess... You think she going to fuck with a nigga?" he asked.

Laney shrugged with a crumbled face. "Ain't no damn telling. You know them Cartel types though. She's a fucking psychopath with no filter at all. If she doesn't like you, trust me, she'll make it known."

"That bitch better not get disrespectful because you know how I am. I don't fold for nobody!" he spat firmly.

Laney rolled her eyes again. "Even if y'all don't like each other, y'all are going to behave yourselves on the strength of me!"

CHAPTER 8

LANEY

To Laney's surprise, Karmen texted her an address that was literally walking distance away from Ta'Jae's estate.

"Damn, what's this all about?" Lester asked from the driver's seat of the Sprinter van. It was luxuriously customized on the inside to Laney's liking. "Whose spot is this? This looks just as big as Ta'Jae's shit."

"I know, right? Karmen texted me this address and told me to meet her here. Probably a spot she's just renting for a while. You know how she gets down," Laney answered.

"This some next level shit," Zion stated while looking up at the main mansion with googly eyes.

Laney reached over and placed a gentle hand on his knee. "Don't worry, baby. We going to get us a spot like this sooner than later."

"That part... When we do though, I want that mutha-fucka to look just like this," he agreed before placing his hand on top of hers.

Lester pulled up in front of the main mansion where Karmen's security infested the property. They got out of the van and were met by Armondo's smooth dressed ass.

"If it isn't the little princess!" he greeted brightly before pulling her in for a tight hug and grabbing both sides of her face, so he could land a big kiss on her forehead.

Laney smiled warmly. "Hi, Uncle 'Mondo... You've already met Lester, but this is my husband, Zion."

Armondo turned to face Zion. "Welcome to the family, young man. My niece speaks the world of you. Nice to meet you."

"Same," Zion responded flatly before shaking Armondo's extended hand. Their eyes were locked, no doubt studying one another.

"You got you a real savage, I see. It's all in his eyes and demeanor. He couldn't hide it if he wanted to... Okay, let's get y'all inside," said Armondo before turning around and leading the way inside the mansion.

Laney was blown away by the architectural design of the place. The inside looked just as beautiful as the outside. It wasn't as big as Ta'Jae's palace, but it definitely had a more modern build. It had to be recently worked on.

"Surpriseeeee!" Karmen and Ta'Jae yelled once they made it into the living area.

A huge sign hung behind them that said, *Welcome home, Laney & Zion!* It threw Laney for a loop. "What's all this?"

"All this is yours, silly!" Karmen informed before tossing Laney a set of keys then tossing Zion a set of his own. "This house is in both of your names. I just bought it last week for you guys to start your new family. My grandkids will need some space to play, plus Mini will be back home soon."

Laney's heart dropped, and her eyes began to tear up immediately to the point where her vision got blurry. She was holding it together until Karmen and Ta'Jae rushed up to her and embraced her. It was then that she broke out into tears. She couldn't hold it in anymore. She'd been busting her ass all her life and fending for herself, so the amount of love from the gesture warmed her heart.

It was deeper than the material aspect though. It wasn't just the house itself but the fact that Karmen was genuine and honestly cared for Laney's wellbeing without any strings attached. She never asked Laney for a thing in return, just loyalty. Laney usually held her composure, but in that moment, she was completely overwhelmed. Her face was buried in Karmen's chest as she cried uncontrollably. She felt like a child in that moment because of her vulnerability.

"It's going to be okay, baby girl. Mami's got you," Karmen assured while stroking Laney's head like a precious doll.

"Girl, you got you a house right down the street from mines, and yours is in your name. That's more than what I can say! You better turn that frown upside down. I bought liquor and all. It's time to turn upppp!" Ta'Jae stated in an attempt to brighten Laney up.

Laney pulled her face out of Karmen's chest and looked up at Ta'Jae. "I'm surprised you even here. I thought you was mad at me about Vanya."

"Yeah, I was for a while. I was in my feelings," Ta'Jae admitted. "But Armondo talked some sense into me... Fuck

Vanya! She chose J-Rock over me, and that's her loss. You a real bitch, and I respect you as a woman, so of course I'm here to celebrate your housewarming! Now, let's turn uppp, girl!"

Ta'Jae poured up the liquor, and Laney hooked her phone up to the eighty-five-inch flat screen TV mounted to the wall, so she could play some music. Karmen went into the kitchen to rush the chef, and the men just took a seat.

"Can you believe this shit, bae? All this is ours," Laney asked, then stated, after taking a seat on Zion's lap.

"This shit crazy. I'm not even going to lie. That was some real nigga shit on her behalf," he noted appreciatively.

"Tell me about it... But let's turn up! You going to drink with me?" she asked hopefully with her bottom lip poked out.

"Yeah, I'll drink a little."

She thanked him with a sloppy kiss on the mouth.

CHAPTER 9

ZION

Zion kept his promise and drank a little liquor, not too much though. He had to stay on point. He was still seated on the couch, watching Laney and Ta'Jae dance in the middle of the living area.

"Come take a walk with me," Karmen commanded lightly. This was her first time speaking to him for the thirty minutes that they'd been there.

Zion looked up at her and studied her eyes. They were a soft hazel color, but she still had a hard stare. He wanted to hear what she had to say though, so he got up and followed her out the back of the house. He couldn't help but admire her backside as she walked in the skintight dress pants. She was well dressed, and it was clear that Laney was adopting her dressing style.

The backyard had a tropical theme with coconut trees, tiki bar, and bridges that were built over creeks of water that led to various waterfalls into the large pool. It was beautiful as hell. It looked like a resort or some shit. Everything was well lit, and the water even had lights in it. It probably looked even better in the daytime.

"So, you're the legendary Zion my daughter's been bragging about all this time, huh?" Karmen asked.

Zion nodded. "Yeah, that's me... She been telling me a lot about you as well."

"I know you probably think I'm crazy treating her like my daughter and all... I just see so much of myself in her, and it's just something about her. I fell in love with her at first sight. She's so adorable and pure in my eyes," Karmen admitted in a genuine tone.

Zion shrugged. "I mean, I'm in love with her my damn self, so I understand for the most part. I don't think either of y'all is crazy. It's clear that y'all both need each other. I'm just glad she finally found her a mother figure, I guess. Just don't hurt her because that's when you're going to have a problem with me, and I'm crazy enough to make a move against you."

Karmen stopped on one of the bridges, and to his surprise, she smiled brightly at him, showing all of her beautiful white teeth. "Oh, I know you are. I did a background check on you. I know all about your track record in the streets and behind bars. I even have my own video copy of your fights in the Death Tournament. Cost me a pretty penny but I had to see it for myself... I'm particularly impressed by how hard you fought though. What exactly were you fighting for in that moment? Like what got you through?"

Zion was thrown off by her response and the fact that she went through the trouble of buying a copy of his fights just so she could study him. It told him a lot about the type of woman she was. "To be honest, I was just fighting for a better life. I had ten more years on my sentence, and Laney told me everything she had going on out here, so I did what I had to do to get out here with her and my mother. I was needed out here, so I just did what I needed to do... Plus, I made sure Laney was there at the tournament for extra motivation. Couldn't go out bad in front of my queen," he finished seriously.

Karmen's smile grew wider. "Awwwww! That's so fucking romantic! Men like you is hard to come by... You remind me of my second, and last, husband."

"What happened to him?" he asked curiously with a raised brow.

"I stabbed him to death in his sleep," Karmen answered with a straight face. There was no remorse or regret in her voice or face.

"Whattt? I thought you said he was a good man. What happened?" he asked, unable to hide his conviction.

"He was cheating on me with one of the maids and got her pregnant. I killed him, her, and the baby. In that order," she answered evenly.

Zion shook his head. "Yeah, yo' ass crazy too." He pointed out amusingly with a half-smile. For some reason, that made him fuck with her even more.

"Look at us with something in common!" Karmen stated brightly before hooking her arm into his. "Okay, son. Let's finish our walk... I hope you're not in bed with Yuteg's family. I understand the bond you made with him behind those walls, and that's cool. He's never leaving that prison, so your relationship with him is cool, but his family is borderline terrorists, and we don't need that type of heat.

That's CIA level type shit, which is a whole different can of worms."

Zion's face crumbled up as he quickly shook his head side to side. "Hell nah! I don't fuck with them crazy ass folks. Yuteg's my nigga, but I wouldn't even fuck with them folks even if he allowed me. I'm going legit with this boxing shit. I wouldn't risk it... Bad enough my wife is a whole ass queenpin on the low."

She gave him a surprised look. "What do you mean *if he let you*? He forbade you from dealing with his family?"

Zion nodded.

"Damn. I never knew Russians had hearts. He obviously cares about you," she assessed.

Zion nodded again. "Yeah, let's just say he's the father figure I never had. Sort of like you and Laney but the love is wayyyy tougher."

"I respect that... I like you though, Zion. I can tell you're going to make my daughter a happy woman for many years to come. Just don't get the maid pregnant," she joked seriously.

"I got you," he answered with an amused expression.

CHAPTER 10
TORY

THE NEXT AFTERNOON, TORY WAS DEEP IN ONE OF HIS favorite strippers, Sexy. She was a light skinned baddie in his eyes. She was property of BBG and was loyal to the gang, so he often brought her to his main house to beat that pussy up. He didn't do well with relationships, so he would kidnap one of his favorite local strippers every other weekend, and this weekend it was Sexy's turn. She was the only one that got to see his house though.

He sat on the edge of his bed, leaning back on his elbows, watching her massive, but artificial, ass cheeks clap on his dick. He didn't care that the ass was fake. The doctor did a good job because that muthafucka felt — and looked — **real**.

"Damn, bitch! You throwing that ass backkk tonight!" he complimented while pouring some more oil onto her ass to keep it shiny how he liked it.

"You like that shit, nigga?" she asked as she slowed her rhythm while he rubbed the oil on her ass.

His phone rang, but he ignored it and kept his focus on the jiggly ass at his disposal. Business could wait until after the nut he was building up. He smacked her ass and pulled her long ponytail weave with his free hand.

"Dayyyummmm, nigggaaa!" she spat as she began to squirt uncontrollably. "That's my fourth orgasm, nigga! How many beans did you take?" she asked after standing up, giving herself a break from his dick.

"Bitch, don't worry about it. Get yo' ass back on this dick. I'm about to cum in a minute," he barked seriously with his dick in his hand, staring daggers up at her. He had taken four Ecstasy pills, and they had his dick hard like he'd taken two Viagras.

His phone rang again.

"See, you got business to handle and all. Give a bitch a break. This pussy is going to be here when you get back," Sexy pleaded hopefully.

Tory clenched his teeth and sighed. "Just sit on my face while I jack this dick then. I got to get this nut off me before I do anything," he compromised before laying back on the bed.

She hurried up and climbed on top of him before he changed his mind. She parked that big ass on his face, and he buried his face in it as he began to jack his dick. Maybe that was what he needed because he came in less than three minutes, and he came hard too. It took him another three minutes to gain the strength to get out of the bed and clean himself up.

He took a quick shower, threw on some sweats and a shirt, then checked his phone. Choppa had called him four more times while he was in the shower.

"What the fuck this nigga want?" he asked himself as he returned the call. "It better be important. You know I'm over here with Sexy, nigga!" he spat once Choppa answered the phone.

"Nigga, you know I wouldn't disturb you if it wasn't serious... I found out who been doing business in Fayetteville," Choppa informed with satisfaction in his voice.

"Who?" Tory asked while putting on his socks.

"That hoe, Careesha, that's running Lillington for us."

Tory shook his head. He actually liked Careesha. It was a shame it had to be her. "Damn, where she at?"

"Shit, she in my trunk," Choppa answered nonchalantly. "You told me to bring her straight to you, right? I'm on the way to you now."

"Yeah, man. I'm at my house. Just text me when you here so I can open the garage," he commanded before ending the call.

———

I t took Choppa about an hour to make it to Tory's house. By then, Tory had gotten his dick sucked by Sexy one last time and sent her home early. He had business to handle, and she was a major distraction at the moment.

Choppa backed his dark blue Cadillac XTS into the garage and turned his music down as he did. Once he was parked, he hopped his Black ass out of the car and made his way around the back of the car where Tory was waiting patiently.

"Pop the trunk," Tory instructed before popping another

Ecstasy pill into his mouth. He'd been keeping impossible hours lately, and the pills gave him the fuel he needed to operate for as long as he did.

Choppa pressed the button on his key, and the trunk popped. Careesha popped up out of the trunk like a grasshopper, but Tory was quick with his reaction. He grabbed Careesha around her small neck and threw her onto the ground. "Bitch, calm the fuck down!"

"What the fuck, Tory? What the fuck is this all about? I been in the trunk for hours. I pissed on my fucking self and all! Now you standing there telling me to calm down? Fuck you, nigga!" Careesha spat frantically.

She was just a little taller than Laney, standing at 5'2". She looked like a sweet little ghetto princess, but she was one of the feistiest bitches that Tory knew. She was way past feisty at that moment though; she was livid.

"You fucked up, Careesha," Tory informed while motioning for Choppa to help her up. "You knew not to do business in Fayetteville, but you set up not one but five traps in their city. I thought you was smarter than that."

"Man, it's not enough money around my way, and I wasn't really in Fayetteville if you want to be technical. I was in Spring Lake with it," she answered while leaning on the car. She was out of breath.

Tory shook his head. "Well, I guess that's too close because Donny gave us a call about the shit, and he wasn't happy at all."

"This some bullshit," she spat with a mug.

"Just chill though. You lucky I fuck wit your lil' ass. I'm going to spare your life, but you going to owe me a big personal favor after this."

CHAPTER 11

LANEY

LANEY ENJOYED THE NIGHT AT HER NEW HOUSE WITH HER husband. She wanted to spend the day there with him as well but couldn't because the streets were calling, and she'd be damned if she brought her work stress to her home, so she scheduled all her meetings for the day at her second office. She dropped Zion back off at their condo before having Lester take her to Missy's massage parlor about twenty minutes away, just outside of the downtown area.

It was a nice discreet location, right off of a main street, in a small two-story building. It was the perfect place for Missy to run her operation. It wasn't a Ta'Jae palace or the Static Lounge, but it was something, and it worked for now. The girls were happy, and the customers were happy. That was all that mattered.

"I see business is good around this way," Lester noted, judging from all the nice cars parked in the small, gated parking lot. He had to search for a spot.

Laney smiled. "Yeah, pussy's going to sell more than anything. These bitches making me more money than ever... Just park in front of the building. This my shit anyway."

Lester obliged, and Laney hopped out of the van. She looked like a snack with her tan mini dress and white blouse. She strolled into the establishment and was greeted super brightly by the receptionist. "Bossss laddyyyy! You slaying that fit, girlll!"

"Thank you, baby... Where's Missy?"

"She's out for the night. She took Debo out on a date. You want me to call her up here?"

Laney shook her head. "Nah, let them enjoy themselves. I'm not here for her anyway. I'm going to my office, and I'm expecting some guests. Just show them to my office as they come and cut them cameras off until I leave... Oh, yeah... Get one of our best girls to entertain Lester while he waits," she instructed before making her way to her office in the basement.

Her office at the parlor wasn't as nice as her office at the lounge, but she never spent too much time there anyway, so it didn't really matter. She only used this office for meetings that she couldn't take at the lounge.

Fifteen minutes later, Ice walked into her office with a not-so-happy face. "Big Body has to go! That nigga holding a grudge on me and done robbed me for 3.7 million dollars."

Laney looked up at him with wide eyes. "*Whattt?!*"

"Yeah, I know. That's a lot of fucking money, and I'm not going to let that shit slide," he promised through clenched teeth.

Laney pumped her open palms toward the ground to signal for him to calm down. "Just take a seat and chill for now. He's on the way right now, so he can answer for these allegations," she instructed before Ice reluctantly plopped down in one of her chairs and took a deep breath.

Ten short minutes later, Big Body casually strolled into her office with all his jewelry on. "Damn, nigga, you on your way to one of them raggedy ass bitch houses after this?" she asked.

"As a matter of fact, I am. After I hit the club with the gang... What's this all about?" he asked before taking a seat alongside Ice. They were both facing her.

"Okay. Now, Ice just came in here mad. He say you holding a grudge on him and robbed him for damn near four million dollars. I need to know what the fuck is going on because I thought I made myself clear about this internal beef shit," Laney spat sternly.

Big Body's face crumbled a little. "Four million? Shid-ddd, I wish. The whole world know this nigga's sweet as pie. I don't blame the muthafucka that did it, but it sure wasn't me. Tell this nigga to show some proof how he did last time. Can't just be walking around here throwing around allegations like that, especially not at a made man like me. The fuck?"

Laney nodded sympathetically at Ice. "I mean, he isn't wrong, Ice... Do you have proof of Big Body robbing you or even setting it up? A witness, video, anything?"

"Man, I know it was this nigga. I just know it!" Ice barked defiantly.

"Show the proof then, bitch ass nigga! You sweet, and you got licked. Now you looking for somebody to point the fingers at. Well, them muthafuckas going to get chopped off pointing 'em this way without no proof," Big Body promised, shooting Ice a death stare.

"Y'all tone that shit down in my office! Listen, Ice. You need to launch an investigation or something, so you can get down to the bottom of this. Until then, I'm going to need you to keep your assumptions to yourself. Am I clear?" Laney asked.

Ice nodded his head before popping up out of his chair and storming out of her office.

"He gone cry in the car," Big Body stated amusingly.

Laney couldn't hold in her chuckle. "Shut your ass up, nigga! I better not find out you had anything to do with this."

"I been on a straight and narrow," Big Body promised with crossed fingers.

"Get out of my office," she commanded. "Take your ass on, nigga!"

Big Body was gone, and she was left in the office with her own thoughts. She actually believed that Big Body had something to do with the robbery, but without proof, there wasn't anything even she could do. She knew how slimy Big Body could get, but that wasn't really her problem. As long as he wasn't planning on snaking her, she was good. It probably was on the strength of Zion, but it didn't matter.

Not even a full five minutes later, Tory walked in her office with a small woman.

"So, this the bitch that got Donny calling me talking crazy?" Laney asked as they walked in.

Tory shook his head. "I mean, she running Lillington

for us, and it was one of hers that did it, but it wasn't her specifically."

Laney studied the woman closely. She returned Laney's stare without wavering. "What's your name again?"

"Careesha."

"Okay, Careesha. This is what's going to happen. You're going to go back to your little town and grab whoever's responsible for going against the grain. Then, you're going to bring their asses back up here to me, and I'm going to watch you cut both of their hands off at the wrists. Thennn, you're going to put both of those hands in a cooler of ice and transport them allll the way back to Fayet-teville where one of those DG niggas will be waiting to relieve you of the box... Do I make myself perfectly clear?"

Careesha nodded rapidly.

"Okay, good. Now, get the fuck out of my office," she spat. "Not you, nigga. Stay," she told Tory.

"What I do now, man?" he asked with a half-smile.

"You better wipe that fucking smile off your face. You and Big Body think y'all so fucking clever. I'm glad Zion didn't turn out like y'all sneaky bastards. I don't even know why he like y'all so much," she spat with a grimace.

"Because we all been through some shit growing up together... Where all that's coming from though?" he asked curiously.

"Body know what he did. I'm sure he'll tell you since y'all muthafuckas so tight, and I feel like you just covered for that bitch. She's guilty as hell. I seen it all in her eyes, but lucky for you, and Body, I'm not petty like J-Rock. I don't give a fuck about none of this shit to be honest. I'm just here to make this shit look good and get my money in the process."

"Oh, I'm already knowing how you rocking, sis."

She rolled her eyes. "Sis my ass... Y'all better not get too comfortable bending these rules though because if it catches up to any one of y'all, you going to regret it."

"Just chill. I got shit under control, and I'm damn sure Big Body got his shit under control. Ain't nothing to worry about, Boss Lady," Tory promised before confidently strolling out of the office.

"Uhmmm hmmm! Fuck around and be the first to die. Keep on playing with my intelligence, nigga," she mumbled once he was gone.

CHAPTER 12

GLOCK

"So, LOCAL AUTHORITIES ARE HAVING A TOUGH TIME AT the moment. The two officers, who were involved in the teenage shooting just two days ago, are both officially reported missing. Some speculation has arisen that they both fled, so they wouldn't have to deal with the repercussions of the unlawful shooting, and others believe that they've been kidnapped by local gangbangers. Neither theory has been confirmed as of yet. The only fact that can be confirmed, so far, is that both officers are indeed missing... Both were last seen at a local bar last night, drinking and talking together, but neither of them made it home to their families that night. There's no evidence or witnesses to a kidnapping, which is why most believe they fled to avoid inevitable jail time..." Glock shut off the TV.

He turned to look at Ruga, who sat next to him on his couch. "What you think, nigga?"

"I think that nigga, Murk, is a fucking genius," Ruga admitted with a smirk. "He was right. That was the perfect way to go about the shit. We killed two birds with one stone. Got our revenge and kept the heat off of us. Can't ask for no better outcome, gang."

Glock nodded his agreement. As much as he hated to admit it, he was dead ass wrong with the initial approach he was trying to take. Shit would've gotten very ugly had he made the example he wanted to make.

"Now, all we got to do is spread rumors on Facebook and Instagram. Get some of them girls in the hood that know how to make the meme pictures and shit. We got to go viral with them shits. They went from serving justice to running from justice. That's the slogan we got to push." He plotted aloud.

Ruga rubbed his hands together in prayer position. "I see Murk ain't the only genius. That's a good idea right there. I'm on it," Ruga assured before getting up and leaving the apartment.

"So, you just not going to say shit? I know yo' ass ain't sleep over there," he said to his mother, who was laying comfortably on the other couch. She hadn't said a word to anyone since finding out about Ja'Kiya's death. All she did was cry, eat, and lay down in her pajamas. She was like a zombie. "I got 'em, Mama. I know that won't bring her back, but at least I got they asses. They won't hurt nobody else though, and it send a warning to the rest of them racist ass muthafuckas," he assured comfortingly.

She didn't say a word still. She just sighed and rolled over into the couch, so her ass was hanging off of the couch and her back was to him. There was nothing he could do for her but give her time to heal, even though he didn't have that same luxury. He had an empire to run.

CHAPTER 13

LANEY

LATER ON THAT EVENING, LANEY SWUNG BY THE LOUNGE before she took it in for the night. It was *Old School Monday,* and she liked the vibe that the older crowd brought. She got herself a VIP section and ordered some champagne for herself, so she could wind down after a long day on the throne. She took a seat on the sofa, and Lester stood guard at the entrance of the section.

"Look at you out here like a civilian," Craig joked as he delivered her a sparking bottle of champagne personally.

He sat with her and poured them both glasses of champagne. "You here to enjoy this old school vibe, huh? This your second Monday in a row."

"Yuuup!" she agreed, full of animation. "Had a long and stressful day. Just need to wind down."

"Where you coming from? Your other office?"

"Yeappp," she answered before taking a sip of her glass.

"You seen Debo? What he got going on over there? Still on Missy's bra strap?"

Laney laughed. "You know he's in love with that bitch. I'm glad I put him on her security detail though. They're literally perfect for each other."

"My nephew done fell in love with a hoe," Craig joked while shaking his head.

Laney punched him on the shoulder. "Don't do my bitch! Missy is a solid bitch and will kill or die behind hers. He the lucky one if you ask me."

"Yeah, yeah, yeahhh!" Craig blurted childishly. "On some real shit though, you're going to have to wrap this up though. I got an important party on the way, and I need this VIP section for them. Plus, there's a surprise waiting for you in your office."

"Didn't I tell you to stay out of my shit, nigga?" she spat with furrowed brows.

Craig raised his hands in surrender. "I ain't stepped a foot in there ever since. Like I said, the surprise is in there waiting on you."

"You too old to be playing games, man... What's up there?" she demanded.

"Not what but who."

She shot him a death stare before getting up and shooting up to her office. She was curious as to who the fuck was in her shit. The only person she could think of was Zion trying to surprise her with some dick at work.

She made it upstairs and opened the door to her office, expecting to find Zion naked on her couch or something, but the man that was sitting behind her desk made her heart drop. He was one of the sexiest and realest men she'd ever had the pleasure of knowing. He sat there in a grey three-piece suit and his long, perfect box braids. The nigga looked like he was born in a *GQ* magazine. She was frozen like a statue at the door, completely shocked.

"Looking good in that mini dress, girl. That sophisticated look does you some real muthafuckin' justice for real... Spin around for me one time."

Laney blushed and did a little twirl for him. "You always doing the mostttt!"

"Only with the people I really care about... Come, take a seat. Talk to me," Static instructed warmly.

Laney obliged without a second thought. "What you doing here? You could've just called or something. It's been yearsssss since I've seen you. We could've went out and did something special or something."

He shook his head. "You know how I am. I have fun different than most people. Just me sitting right here across from you is fun. Plus, I'm just in and out the city. Had to close a major deal face-to-face. My flight leaves in two hours though, but I had to see you before I left... Heard you got a lot on your plate these days."

"You been talking to J-Rock, huh?" she asked with a roll of her eyes. She couldn't help it. The nigga still made her cringe, just by the thought of him.

Static nodded his answer with a smirk. "Of course. That's my brother."

"I still don't see how two niggas so different can be so close. I've spent time around both of y'all, and I still can't figure it out," she admitted for the first time.

"Me and J-Rock done been through some shit together.

He saved my life, and I gave him a better life. It's a lot of shit in between, but that sums it up."

"I guess."

Static studied her for a while before replying. "How you been holding up though? He told me *everything* that's been going on, and I'm sorry you had to endure all that. Even sorrier that I couldn't protect you from it. Just glad you came out on top."

"I don't blame you. At the end of the day, you gave me a better life than I would've had. All the bullshit I endured is just me having to pay my taxes to the universe. That's how I look at it," she replied seriously.

Static nodded his understanding. "Either way, I'm proud of you and the woman you've become. You're holding shit down, and the whole empire is on your back now. I wasn't able to keep you from the streets like I promised, so I figured I'd make up for it. Whether you blame me or not, I still feel bad. You had a pass out the streets, and J-Rock forced you back in for life. You're the perfect person for the position, so I couldn't even blame him, but I had to do something."

"What you do, Static?" she asked curiously with a raised brow.

"That deal I just closed was for the amusement park I'm having built, and fifty percent of that is legally yours. That will accumulate to millions of dollars a year once it's up and running. Just something positive to add to your legacy to make it harder for the Feds to touch you."

Tears began to well up in her eyes. The devil was obviously working, but the fact that God was working too gave her hope that shit would get better. It was fuel to keep pushing forward on her journey. "I love you, nigga! You always been solid. I never deserved you in my life."

He stood up to his full six-foot height and fixed himself up. "Stop the foolishness. You're an angel in my eyes. I don't care what anybody else thinks, including yourself... I have to hit the road now, just keep surviving and prospering how you been doing. I'll be in touch," he stated before heading out of the office.

She shot up out of her seat and spun around. "So, I don't get a hug or nothing? Lord knows when the next time I'll see you."

He stopped in his tracks, right at the door, and turned toward her with a knowing expression. "It's been a while but not long enough to where you forgot what I always used to tell you before I went ghost... I can't put my hands on you because I'll never want to take them off," he recited before disappearing like the ghost he now was.

Laney bit her bottom lip as she leaned back on her desk and caught her breath. As usual, that nigga left her with short breath and wet panties. She never could help herself around his smooth ass, and even now, with Zion in the picture, it was still the same.

It was best that Static was never around because the undercover chemistry they shared wasn't healthy for either of them. As a matter of fact, the older she got, the more she understood why Static didn't like to spend too much time around her. He was faithful to his wife, and she made it hard for him. Now that she had a husband, she could relate more.

CHAPTER 14

ICE

ICE WAS STUCK BETWEEN A BOULDER AND A SLAB OF concrete. He was down millions of dollars, and knew exactly who was behind it, but couldn't prove it. Whoever robbed his house wore a mask and gloves, so they couldn't be identified. Not many knew where he lived though, so that meant he was followed or was betrayed by one of his own. He didn't want to believe the last possibility but had to consider all scenarios. Shit was wicked these days.

He found himself at the front door of Murk's high-rise apartment. It was just after noon, and he tried to call ahead, but Murk wasn't answering his phone.

"What's up?" Murk's baby mother asked with a hint of attitude.

"Murk's not answering his phone, and Laney said he wasn't out of town, so I figured he was here," Ice replied hopefully.

Anaria rolled her eyes. "Yeah, he here, but you might

want to try him another time because he ain't in the best of moods right now."

"It's urgent. I need to talk to him now. It won't take long," he stated in a pleading tone.

She shrugged her boney shoulder and stepped aside. "Go ahead. I tried to warn your ass... He in the room straight to the back on the left."

Ice waved at their daughter, who played in the living room, as he made his way back there. She waved back at him before he disappeared into the hallway. He walked back to the room and knocked on the door twice.

"Yeahhh!" Murk spat from the other side of the door. Ice could tell he wasn't in the mood.

When he opened the door, he could see that Murk wasn't in the mood. Not at all. He laid on their carpeted floor in nothing but a pair of basketball shorts, halfway balled up. "You alright down there?" Ice asked out of curious concern.

Murk looked up at Ice. "Fuck you doing here? And do it look like I'm alright, nigga? My stomach fucked up. Think that dirty bitch tried to poison a nigga."

"I got a dilemma, and I need your help," he answered, purposely ignoring the part about him getting poisoned. That wasn't his business, and he had nothing to say about it.

"What dilemma, Ice?" Murk asked irritably, clutching his stomach.

Ice took a deep breath. "My house just got robbed for damn near four million dollars, and I think Big Body was behind it. I need you to find out if it really was him. I'll pay you reallll good."

"Nigga, you better hire a private investigator or some shit. I'm the executioner. So, if you know the nigga did it, but can't prove it, and still want him dead, we can have a talk for the right price. I ain't in the business of investigation though. I torture shit," Murk informed though clenched teeth, clearly being tortured by his stomach at the moment.

Ice sighed. "I know Big Body was behind it. He been out to get me ever since I had two of his taken out."

"You want my advice, fool?"

"I'm not here for advice, but I'll take it," said Ice.

"It's a reason why most scammers live they life on the road, bruh," he said before pausing to grimace. It looked like a wave of pain was washing over him. "Y'all niggas some walking licks. If you on the move, it make it harder for niggas like Big Body to plot on you... Get your crew and get the fuck out of Charlotte because this shit is going to get a lot worse before it get better."

Ice stood there, thinking about Murk's words, but his pride wasn't trying to hear that shit. "Like I said, I know he did it, and I doubt I'll be able to prove the shit, knowing that nigga. He slimy but clever. Sooooo, what you going to charge me to make him disappear?"

"If I do decide to do it, I'm going to need a quarter million. That's a high-profile ass body right there and a high fucking risk."

"I'll give you double that if you kill him slowly," Ice informed urgently. "I swear I hate that nigga."

"I'll think about it, Ice. I'll let you know soon."

Ice smirked as a wave of relief washed over him. "I appreciate that for real, bruh."

"Now get the hell out. Let me deal with this pain in peace."

CHAPTER 15

BIG BODY

Big Body sat in the bleachers, watching Zion spar with two boxers against him — one heavyweight and the other light heavyweight. It was an advanced training technique that conditioned the fighter under impossible situations. One fighter had excessive strength, and the other had excessive speed, but Zion was holding his own. It was a lose-lose situation, but the better Zion got at fighting two fighters at the same time, the worse off a single opponent would be up against him solo.

Big Body used to box with Zion when they were little, so he was hip to the sport and all the formalities. Zion just kept boxing a lot longer than he had because he got locked up when they were in their early teens. By the time he got out of juvenile, he was neck deep in the streets and didn't have room for boxing, but Zion stuck to it, all the way until he finally got locked up at the age of twenty. He just never pursued a professional career until now.

"Turn up the heat! Y'all stop holding back! Fight him

like y'all fighting a grizzly bear," the trainer barked at Zion's opponents.

Zion held his own as his two opponents showed him no mercy. Big Body was amazed every time he saw Zion in action. Prison gave him more savageness to his fighting style. He noticed Zion start to spin, but he dropped his elbow at the last second.

The trainer didn't miss it. "Leave that wild shit in the prison cell where you picked it up at. This is boxing! No knees or elbows. If you want me to sign you up with UFC, just let me know!"

Big Body clenched his teeth because he could feel the frustration steaming off of Zion. He was restraining himself from going into savage mode, and it was noticeable. He did the best he could, but the opponents tore his ass up.

After the sparring match, Big Body walked up to the ring and joined Zion in his corner. "You probably should go the UFC route because you done turned into a wild ass fighter. Them niggas wouldn't have stood a chance if you was using them elbows and knees."

"Hell nah!" Zion spat in between breaths, his arms resting on the ropes. "UFC fighters don't get paid shit compared to high-level boxing. I'm getting twenty million for this first fight if I win. Five million if I lose... That's twenty million guaranteed off of my first fight then. You know how many UFC fights it's going to take you to make a fraction of that?"

Zion was right too. ESPN — and all other major sports networks — were all over this fight. Everybody wanted to know who the mysterious ex-convict was that was challenging one of the most feared men in this boxing era. It wasn't usual for a man to go from a jail cell straight to a championship fight, but Zion's management team made it happen. Diehard sports fans from all over the world were anticipating this fight and were willing to pay top dollar to see it, and that was exactly why Zion was getting paid so much money. He was willingly challenging a fighter that no one had been willing to fight for three years as his debut match. It shook the boxing world up, and he clearly planned on capitalizing off of it.

With all that in mind, Big Body nodded his head understandingly. "When you put it like that, it make a lot more sense."

One of Zion's handlers rushed over to him. "A handful of reporters outside want an exclusive. I told them to give you a few minutes."

"Yeah, give me about five more minutes. Let me chop it up with my brother real quick," Zion stated before wiping his sweaty face with a towel.

"You about to blow up like 50 Cent in the early 2000s the way you been trolling the league. Then, after they see you in action and how you back all that shit up, you automatically going down as one of the greats. You about to make history, bruh," Big Body predicted.

Zion nodded. "You damn skippy, and it's only going to get better after this first fight."

"Exactly... That's why after the first fight, you need to convince Laney, to convince J-Rock, that Tory is ready to take over the nation, so y'all can live happily ever after. I know you want her out of that life because this shit is going to get even more wicked, and she's losing more and more of herself by the day. This life snatch your soul away, bruh. You know that," Big Body strategically stated.

He knew with Tory in charge of things, he'd have free reign to do just about whatever. He'd basically be in charge of himself because Tory was his evil twin. He knew how much Zion cared for Laney, so he wouldn't kill her. This was his best play toward removing Laney and manipulating his way to the very top of the food chain.

"So, you think J-Rock will go for that? She made it seem like he want her in that shit for life," Zion stated then stated intensely.

Big Body pressed his lips and shook his head. "Nah, man. She probably ain't word it right, but I know for a fact J-Rock will let her go if she assure him that Tory ready to take over. Just throw him a few million dollars on top of that and that'll solidify her retirement papers."

Zion nodded his head slowly while staring into space. "That ain't a bad idea, my nigga. I definitely would sleep better knowing my lil' baby safe every day. Especially since she pregnant now."

"Whattttttt!" Big Body said with wide eyes. He was shocked.

"Yeah, muthafucka... Keep that to yourself though. You the only one that know outside of her godmother. If you run your mouth, me and you going to have problems, nigga," Zion warned very seriously.

Big Body raised his hands in surrender. "Secret safe with me, playa... Just make sure you win this muthafuckin' fight. Like on some overkill type shit. Make a statement and embarrass that nigga. Have folks scared to fight yo' ass after this."

The reporters and cameras were being escorted into the gym by his management team as Big Body finished saying what he had to say. Zion immediately stood up and began to put on a show for the cameras as he leaned on the top rope, peering down at the cameras with a grimace. "I swear on everything I love; I'm going to embarrass that man in the ring. Like I'm not even exaggerating either. I'm going to be the one boxers scared to step in that ring with after this."

"Emmanuel Sanchez says that you're just using the publicity to your advantage and will be happy to take the five million to get knocked out by him. What do you have to say about that?" a petite, blonde lady asked smugly. It was clear that she believed Emmanuel.

Big Body looked up at Zion and wondered what his response would be. Knowing Zion, he had a snappy come-back at the tip of his tongue.

"I feel like a lot of folks believe that too, including you... So, this is what I'm going to do. I want to propose that we up the stakes. *All or nothing!* Winner walks away with twenty-five million dollars, and the loser walks away with nothing! Now, go ask him what he thinks about that," he retorted cockily and returned to his seat in his corner.

The reporters went crazy, frantically shooting question after question, but Zion had said what he said and was obviously done talking for the day. He motioned for his team to get the reporters out of the gym, and just like that, they were gone.

Zion looked over at Big Body with a smirk. "What you think?"

"You a westside baby fasho! Always taking shit to the

extreme," Big Body answered with a smirk of his own while shaking his head. "You got to win now, nigga. I know that nigga going to accept the offer. He can't turn it down."

"This going to be the quickest twenty-five million you *ever* seen a nigga make," Zion promised with a serious expression now.

Big Body had no choice but to believe in his nigga if he believed in himself that much. A slow, devilish grin spread across his face as a new scheme popped up in his head, a scene that Zion had just motivated.

CHAPTER 16

LANEY

"I KNOW YOU FUCKING LYING!" LANEY SPAT IN disapproval. "You and that muthafuckin' pride of yours, man. You just took the safety net from up under you. That was five million dollars you was going to get no matter what."

Zion looked dead at her from the other end of the phone's camera with the most serious face. "Fuck that safety net. I'm going to beat that man to sleep... I'm surprised that you even concerned after seeing me in action. You supposed to have all the faith in the world in me at this point."

"Nigga, please. Of course I have faith in you. It's not about that. This isn't a free for all fight. Boxing has rules, and they have judges that decides the fight, so if you're both still standing at the end of those twelve rounds, it's going to be up to them to decide who wins... All I'm saying is why take away the just in case money," she reasoned.

"Fuck them judges and ain't going to be no just in case.

I'm gon' knock that man the fuck out, and you going to be right there witnessing it, like you was the last time I fought," he predicted confidently.

Laney could tell he believed one hundred percent of every word that he said and just decided to do the same. The damage was already done, so all she could do now was ride with her man and pray for the best possible outcome, like she did last time.

"Alright, baby. Then I guess we going to be some champions then!" she boasted with matching confidence. "Now go ahead and wrap shit up at that gym and bring your ass home. I want to give you a massage or some shit."

He nodded his approval with a slight smirk. "Wait, what home? The condo or the house?"

"The house, nigga! Fuck that condo. We got a whole mansion now. I had all of our shit moved out of there today, and I told Missy she could move in there."

"Alright. I'll be there soon," he promised before blowing her a kiss and ending the video call.

Laney sighed once he was gone. She took a seat on one of the moving boxes in their new mega sized master bedroom and pulled up Sanchez's highlights from previous fights on YouTube. That Puerto Rican muthafucka was nothing to play with. It was easy to see why he was so feared in the boxing world. His speed was insane, and he was aggressive on top of that.

She sat there and watched knockout after knockout. Sanchez had twenty-six knockouts and zero losses. His opponent from his last —_and biggest —_fight was still in a coma. That was three years ago. No fighter had been willing to step in the ring with him ever since up until now. Zion was a huge underdog, but Laney had faith in her man.

Flashbacks of Zion's fights in the tournament began to flood her mind, and she began to smile. Her man was a fucking savage, and if he could beat those odds, that Sanchez muthafucka didn't stand a chance. She had watched Zion fight in multiple life or death matches. He had experience Sanchez didn't. It was with that realization that she stopped worrying about the fight.

Zion was about to shock the world, and like he said, she would be right by his side.

CHAPTER 17
GLOCK

GLOCK RODE IN THE PASSENGER SEAT OF A RENTED BLACK Audi SUV. Ruga's ugly ass was at the wheel, and he was pushing that muthafucka down the interstate.

"Slow yo' muthafuckin' ass down, fool. You trying to get us pulled over? Know we got all these guns in this bitch," he spat firmly.

Ruga eased up on the pedal and slowed down closer to the speed limit. "My bad, bruh. This muthafucka so damn smooth. Don't even feel like we was going all that fast."

"Yeah, whateva, nigga. Done left the gang and all. They just now catching up." Glock pointed out while looking at the approaching grey Toyota Camry in the rearview mirror.

Ruga glanced at the rearview himself. "Why we ain't bring more shooters than that? We about to go take over a whole city with six niggas? It's new Glockians in the set that's dying to prove themselves, and you just brought all main shooters."

"How I'm feeling right now, I can go take over that

town by my damn self. Trust me, we got more than enough shooters. And all these army guns I got from Murk going to make it that much more easier. These fuck niggas about to get down or lay the fuck down."

Glock was a natural badass. He was known for his fearlessness and ruthlessness, but shit was different now. He felt a different type of evil building inside of him now, and it was *strong*.

"If you say we got enough, then that's what it is," said Ruga.

Glock looked over at him. "Just chill... This ain't going to take no more than a week."

"Let's do it... Then we get to keep anything we take off our victims as a bonus. I can't wait," Ruga stated with genuine enthusiasm.

"You always ready for some shit," Glock noted with a half-smile.

Ruga shrugged. "You been knowing me for a long time. It's just how I am, shit. Can't help it."

"I ain't complaining, nigga," Glock assured. "Just glad to have a loyal nigga by my side through all this shit we been going thorough over the years."

"Don't get sentimental on me now, nigga," Ruga joked.

"Shut the fuck up and drive, man," Glock instructed before throwing back an Ecstasy pill and leaning back in his seat.

CHAPTER 18

TORY

TORY STOOD IN ONE OF BIG BODY'S MANY STORAGE UNITS around the city. They had just unloaded the counterfeit money into the space. It was plastic wrapped inside of four medium sized moving boxes.

"We got two months until the fight, so I'm just going to hold it here. Just in case Laney have my houses checked or some shit... I could see it in her eyes; she know I'm behind it," Big Body admitted.

Tory shook his head. "She ain't green at all. She been around long enough to know what the fuck is going on by now."

"Exactly, but Ice can't prove shit, so we good."

"You really going to bet four million dollars on Zion?" Tory asked curiously. He couldn't get over that. "I mean, I know Zion dangerous, but did you see that nigga, Sanchez, fights though? You honestly believe Zion don't got at least a small chance of losing?" he asked with logic.

Big Body quickly shook his head with major confidence. "Fuck no! Zion a fucking savage, and he believe in himself like a muthafucka, so I believe in him. I'm behind him all the way. That Sanchez nigga going to have to show me something because Zion might kill that nigga in that ring."

Tory nodded his understanding. He understood where Big Body came from. "I guess I got to ride with him too. I got money off him last time. Why stop now?"

"Exactly," Big Body agreed. "And since Zion is the underdog, our money is multiplied by a lot more if Zion TKO the nigga. So, you better load up on this fight because I'm trying to be set for life off this fight."

"That's a bet," said Tory. "In the meantime, you need to watch Ice though. That pale muthafucka is slicker than you think."

Tory had spent more time around him than Big Body had, and he knew what Ice was capable of. He might not have been as aggressive as Big Body, but both of them knew how to get their way when they wanted it, and Tory was sure Ice wanted him dead.

"Fuck, Buddy. He ain't stupid," Big Body retorted. He was obviously unfazed by the thought of Ice. "I need to chop it up with you about some real shit though before we head out."

Tory raised a curious brow. "What?" he asked before taking a seat on a folding chair in the corner, so he could roll his weed.

"Your ass is going to have to get all the way on your shit because you're about to be next up realll soon, bruh," Big Body stated seriously.

Tory squinted at his comrade. "What you mean by that? How you figure?"

"Listen, I'm about to tell you some shit that *can't* be repeated, nigga! If this shit get out, me and you going to have some problems."

"Man, spill the beans!" Tory demanded impatiently. He hated to wonder.

"Laney is pregnant, and I convinced Zion to convince Laney to convince J-Rock to let you take over the nation after the fight," he informed, unable to hide his excitement.

Tory was caught off guard with that one. "Damn... That's a lot of convincing. How you so sure that plan is going to work?"

"Because Zion is going to pay J-Rock millions of dollars to make it happen. J-Rock a lot of things, but the nigga ain't stupid. He ain't turning down no free millions. He know you loyal and got what it takes. He just want to be sure, and Laney going to convince him of that. All your Black ass got to do is stay focused and on top of your shit. You about to have a lot more responsibility real soon."

Tory digested Big Body's words carefully and felt a wave of victory wash over him. Lately, he'd been worried about Laney handing the nation over to Murk, so to be hearing that from Big Body was a major relief. He made a promise to himself right then that he would go twice as hard as he'd been going with his hustle. No more bullshit-ting around.

CHAPTER 19

LANEY

Laney had retired early for the night and was watching the news in her bedroom while waiting for the cook to finish making the seafood boil. Zion laid up under her on his stomach as she massaged his muscular back slowly. He seemed to be enjoying it because he was about halfway sleep.

She looked back up at the TV mounted high on their tall wall and listened to the news reporter cover the story of the two missing officers. Their families were playing victim and demanding that the police department find their loved ones, but there was nothing the police could do because they didn't have a trace to follow. There was no evidence of a kidnapping, so all they could do officially was report them missing.

Glock's mother had finally broken her silence and began to post on social media. She made a heartfelt video earlier in the day demanding that the authorities find the two murderous cops so that they could be brought to justice for the unlawful death of her little girl. She also announced that she would be suing the City of Charlotte and needed a good civil lawyer to assist in the matter. The video quickly went viral on the internet and ended up getting played on the national news. It was a whole thing.

"I hope that nigga, Murk, covered all of his damn tracks," she prayed aloud.

"Huh?" Zion said, sounding like he had just been awakened.

"Nothing, baby. You ready to eat?"

"I'm ready to go see Mini. I want to see my daughter asap. Just had a dream about her little ass," he informed urgently.

She gave him a sweet look, even though he couldn't see it. "Awww, she'll be home in a few months, baby."

"Fuck that. I want to see her now. Let's hop on a plane and surprise her in LA. Tory can handle shit while we're gone," he strongly suggested while turning around onto his back, so he could see her.

Laney shrugged her shoulders. "If you say so. I was supposed to visit her anyway, but shit's been hectic. I guess Tory can keep shit under control for a few days... I guess we can head out after we eat that seafood."

"Alright, go ahead and book the flights and shit. You know I don't know how to do all that," he commanded before rolling back over on his stomach.

She rolled her eyes with a smile. She loved when he took control.

CHAPTER 20
GLOCK

They made it to Durham, North Carolina safely the next afternoon. It was a decent country city with a population of about a quarter million people. Their first stop was the nearest rundown motel they could find. It was the first thing on the list when taking over a new city. Glock was sure he could accomplish the mission his way, but Murk had taken over seven cities successfully, so he'd just follow his blueprint.

Murk would've been leading the mission if he wasn't still sick. He told Glock he was going to postpone the meeting, but Glock insisted that he was sent instead. He needed something to keep him busy, and he needed to prove that he was ready for more responsibility. Murk ran the idea up to Laney, who approved it, so Glock had to make sure shit went smoothly. He had to put his emotions aside and use his head.

First thing first, they had to make some friends and throw some money around. He didn't know anything about

Durham, so he had to find out. The best information came from junkies and prostitutes. They knew everything going on in their city and would drop a dime if you dropped a dollar in their hands.

"Bruh, I wish you would stop stalking that girl and get yo' head in the game. If she not responding, then what that tell you? She not interested," Glock told Ruga.

Ruga twisted his lips up. "Nigga, the only reason she be leaving my messages on seen is because I be leaving her speechless with the dope ass shit I be saying."

That made Glock laugh involuntarily. Ruga was funny as hell when he wanted to be. "I can't wit you, bruh. Take your ass out there and bring a few of them junkies back with you."

Ruga sent one last message out before leaving the motel room with one of the shooters. Once they were gone, Glock turned toward the other three shooters. "Y'all go grab us something to eat and hurry back."

They got up and left without hesitation or protest. Glock plopped down on one of the dusty beds and enjoyed the brief moment of solitude. He pulled out his phone and finished watching the video his mother had posted the day before. It was up to nearly two million views and climbing.

She had broken her silence in a public way, and Glock appreciated her for pushing the agenda. The more people that believed the officers were on the run, the better. Glock got his lick back, and the world would never know, but that was cool with him. The people that mattered knew, and his little sister knew.

Ruga was back in no time with two crack heads, two older, Black men. One looked like he fixed cars, with the dirty overalls on, and the other one looked like he used to be something like a pimp back in his day with his colorful, fitted suit on.

"They both from here and trying to make some money," Ruga informed before plopping down on the other bed.

"Y'all trying to get some money, huh?" Glock asked the fiends, who were still standing by the door.

They nodded in unison.

"I got a hundred dollars apiece for y'all, but I'm going to need accurate information though. If I find out y'all old fuckers just told me anything for my money, I'm going to hunt y'all down and get a hundred screams out of y'all for every dollar y'all hustled me out of," he threatened seriously.

The broke down pimp raised his hands in surrender. "Woah, babyyy! Ain't no need for the screams because I swear this shit ain't what it seems. You know what I mean?" He was obviously the slick one.

"How many gangs run this city?" Glock asked curiously.

"Well, out here, it's all about race really. All of the whites stick together, and the Blacks do the same. Especially since we're the minority. Those Aryan Brotherhood devils got the Choppa Family outnumbered three to one. So, they don't have a choice but to stick together."

Glock nodded his understanding. "Okay, cool. Who runs the Choppa Family, and where can I find them?"

"A smooth dude called Dang. He used to be married to one of my nieces. Just a little taller and lighter than me... He lives across town in a big house, but you can find him in Forestcrest Apartments about twenty minutes from here. It's their main headquarters," the other man informed.

Glock nodded. "Okay... I can work with that information. It better be accurate, like I said. Pay 'em, Ruga."

Ruga gave them both a hundred-dollar bill apiece and sent them on about their way. "So, what now?"

"Now, we stalk our prey."

CHAPTER 21
LANEY

Laney and Zion's first-class Delta flight was scheduled for four o'clock that evening, and she had to take care of a little business before then. She held the meeting at Tory's house since it was his problem.

Lester drove her there, and Tory met her in the driveway. "Damn, been waiting on you for an hour."

"You'll be alright," she retorted matter-of-factly. "Where's Careesha?"

"In the shed. Didn't want the mess in my basement. Follow me," said Tory before leading the way around his house and to his backyard where his large shed sat.

When they entered the shed, Careesha stood over a middle-aged man in a black Dickies jumpsuit. A brand-new machete was in her gloved hands, and she had a grimace on her face, obviously not comfortable with the task ahead of her.

"Turn him over. Let me see the nigga's face," Laney

instructed her. The middle-aged man was tied at the wrists and ankles.

Careesha flipped the man over, and Laney looked in his lifeless eyes that stared at the ceiling. "Is he dead already?"

"Yeah," Tory answered. "He was going to die anyway, so I just choked the nigga out, so we wouldn't have to hear all that unnecessary screaming and shit."

"Did I tell you to kill him? What if I wanted to talk to the nigga?" she spat. "Hurry up and chop the nigga's hands off, so I can go, chile," she told Careesha in an agitated tone.

Careesha took a few deep breaths before bending down and doing the deed. She was a bloody mess by the time she was done.

"Good job. Now, go buy a small cooler, put them shits on ice, take 'em to Fayetteville, and give it to the first DG nigga you see. Just tell them that's for Donny, and your job is done... Don't let no shit like this happen again. Stay on your turf," she commanded before exiting the smelly shed. Tory was right behind her.

"I'm going to be gone for a few days. You're in charge, Tory. Keep shit tight and stay on top of all the business."

"Come on now. You ain't even have to say all that. I'm going to handle the business fasho," he assured matter-of-factly.

"Alright." They were back in front of the house, walking down the driveway, where Lester held the truck door open for her. "Go help that girl with that body. You done helped her with everything else," she stated purposely, letting Tory know that she was hip to him sparing her life.

Tory couldn't even respond with one of his usual witty

comebacks this time. He just shook his head with a chuckle and walked off back down the driveway.

"Everything good?" Lester asked as she climbed into the truck.

"Yuuup!" she assured after he closed the door behind her and hopped into the driver's seat. "Now, take me to my husband."

———

L aney and Lester met Zion at the airport where they all boarded the plane together. The first-class section was spacious and elegant. Laney and Zion sat next to each other, and Lester sat across from them.

She looked over at Zion, who had his seat reclined and his feet up, as he took a much-needed nap. Her poor man had been training his ass off lately and deserved the brief vacation. The fatherly love he had for Mini and the bond they shared melted her heart. Laney was just going to wait until Mini made it back to go see her, but the fact that Zion missed her so much that he couldn't wait meant a lot to her.

She looked over at Lester, who was watching a movie on his phone. She was fatigued herself, so she reclined her own seat and shut her eyes. She immediately began to reflect on her life. She didn't know if it was the pregnancy or what, but she'd been looking at life a lot differently lately and speaking to God a lot more.

Despite her being cursed with the burden of running Rock Nation, she couldn't complain at all. She was wealthy, with a beautiful family of her own, and her man was finally home. It seemed like all of her sacrifices had been worth it, and that was all that mattered. She had no regrets and thanked God every chance she got. She might not have been dealt the best cards in the deck, but she was making sure her kids got dealt royal flushes.

It wasn't until right then that she realized she needed the mini vacation just as much as Zion. She'd been consumed in the underworld for all this time, and it felt good to take a breath of fresh air for a change. At that moment, she wasn't a queenpin managing a major criminal organization. She was a wife and a mother, who was visiting her lovely daughter.

A slow smile grew on her face.

CHAPTER 22

MURK

MURK WAS STILL SPENDING MORE TIME ON THE TOILET than usual, but at least the stomach pains were gone. He was currently sitting on the toilet when his baby mother walked in on him. "Bitch, didn't I tell you to start knocking on the door before you walk in on a nigga?"

She rolled her big eyes and put a hand on her small waist. "Nigga, knock for what? I done smelled your shit before... Swiss is here for you."

"Tell him to wait for me in the living room. I'll be out in a minute," he instructed before throwing a roll of tissue at her that clocked her dead in the face. "Now, get the fuck out."

She threw the tissue back at him, that he caught in his hands, and ran her little ass out of the bathroom before he could throw it back.

"Dumb ass," he said with a disappointed shake of his head.

Murk finished up in the bathroom, threw on a tank top, and headed into the living room to meet Swiss. "Wassup, lil' bruh?" he asked as he entered the living room and sat in his comfy chair.

"Shit, everything been on pause since you been out of commission. I been keeping the Vultures on the training schedule, but other than that, I just told them niggas to do they own things until further notice," Swiss answered from the couch.

"Cool, cool. Them niggas needed a lil' break anyway... I called you over here because I need to run something by you though. I need your opinion."

Swiss gave him a funny look, favoring Murk a little bit minus the grey eyes. "Whatttt? You need an opinion? I think that's a first right there. You ain't the type to ask for opinions for real."

"Exactly. I'm really not, but this situation is real delicate," he admitted before giving Swiss the whole rundown on the hit Ice wanted to put on Big Body and the reason why.

"Damnnnn. That nigga, Big Body, greasy as hell."

Murk nodded in agreement. "All them BBG niggas is. It's in they nature... What you think though? Think I should take the heat?"

Swiss shook his head rapidly. "Hell no! Maybe four years ago when we needed the money. We super straight now. That shit not worth the risk because if the pressure get put on Ice, he going to melt and give us up. Fuck that shit, dawg."

"Yeah, you actually making a lot of sense right now."

"I know, nigga. So, tell that nigga to do it himself if he want it done so badly. Nigga got like five bodies on his belt and ain't commit none of 'em. Well, now it's time to see what he really made of."

Murk nodded with a sinister grin. "Yeah, let's see."

CHAPTER 23

GLOCK

GLOCK WAS SMART ENOUGH NOT TO TRY AND MAKE A MOVE on Dang inside of Forestcrest Apartments. It was street nigga 101 to wait him out. They threw some more money around and found out what Dang was driving in. They parked at the very front of the apartment complex, and when they finally saw a dark blue Chevy pickup exiting the complex, they followed.

They followed him all the way to his house on the other side of town and kept driving past after he turned into his driveway. It was a nice suburban neighborhood, not mansions but nice sized houses though. "Ole Dang got a nice lil' set up out here," Ruga noted audibly.

"Yeah, he doing aight for himself. Can't wait to see the inside," Glock responded mischievously.

Four hours later, just short of 3:00 a.m., they doubled back to pay Dang an unexpected visit. They parked their vehicles in the parking lot of a high school that set on the other side of the neighborhood. They loaded up their guns and equipment then headed into the mild patch of woods that separated the high school from Dang's neighborhood. They were all dressed in black from head to toe with hoodies over their heads.

All six of them navigated through the woods in a single file line with Glock leading the pack. He followed the GPS coordinates that showed up on his phone. Once they cleared the woods, they ended up right in Dang's backyard.

"Do your thing, Ruga," Glock instructed.

Ruga's father was a professional burglar and showed Ruga all the tricks to his trade. Ruga's specialty was cutting off the electricity in the house, so they didn't have to worry about the security system. Ruga went ahead and did just that. Three short minutes later, the electricity was off in the house, and two minutes after that, they were slipping through the back door.

"Go bring him, and whoever else, down here to me," Glock instructed before opening the refrigerator, using the flashlight on his phone to see inside.

Ruga and the other four Glockians headed upstairs with their guns drawn, just in case Dang was on point. Glock began to fix himself a sliced ham sandwich while they were gone. He hadn't eaten since earlier and couldn't help it.

"He was up there sleeping by himself. The rest of the house is empty," Ruga informed before hopping on the kitchen counter.

Glock looked up at Dang and aimed the light on him. There was a little light coming from the full moon outside too, so it wasn't totally dark. "Y'all can have whatever y'all want out this muthafucka. I don't want no smoke."

Glock studied his facial expression and tone of voice.

He was alarmed for sure but not exactly frightened. That meant he was familiar with being in that predicament, or he was just good at hiding his feelings.

"And what all do you have in this muthafucka?" Glock asked curiously.

"Everything's in the basement in the deep freezer," he admitted a little too quickly.

Glock nodded at Ruga, who quickly hopped off of the counter and made his way to the basement. Glock went back in the refrigerator to grab some mayonnaise and cheese. He made a healthy sandwich and looked back up at Dang after taking a bite. He flashed the light on Dang, who was noticeably curious about the man who had made a sandwich in his house in the middle of an invasion. He stood there, towering over two Glockians. He was a tall and slim dude, probably in his mid-thirties.

"You gave up that stash pretty quick. Make me feel like you got some more somewhere," said Glock with a mouthful of food.

"Found a block of cash at the bottom of the freezer," Ruga announced with a frozen plastic block of cash in his left hand.

"That's fifty thousand... All I've got," Dang claimed with a straight face.

"I doubt that, but fifty thousand will do for now," Glock assured. "Just think of it as your entry fee into Rock Nation."

Dang's eyes grew a little wider when he realized this was a takeover and not a simple robbery. Everyone in North Carolina knew about Rock Nation's takeovers, and judging by the look on Dang's face, it was clear that he did too. "I always knew it was a matter of time."

"Well, looks like you was always right," Glock retorted after taking another bite of his sandwich. "Now, the question is, are you going to get down or lay down? If you ask me, you might as well get down because if we kill you, somebody else is just going to take your place and get with this shit. It's a battle you can't win."

Dang shrugged smugly. "My nigga, I don't give a damn. I'm cool as long as I'm getting money. I'm not with the power struck shit, but you are talking to the wrong man about all this though. I'm just like a manager out here. You need to be talking business with the real boss."

That statement took Glock by surprise. There he was, thinking he was talking to the big dawg, and the whole time, the real big dawg was behind the scenes somewhere. Glock wanted to meet this muthafucka. "And who is your boss?"

"Pastor Mack," Dang answered. "You can find him at the First Baptist Church around the corner from the apartments you followed me from. His doors is always open, so you won't have to break in. Just simply walk in," he informed with mild sarcasm.

Glock looked at Ruga, who shrugged. Shit just got interesting.

CHAPTER 24
ZION

MINI WAS WAITING FOR THEM AT LAX WHEN THEY LANDED, and she was so excited to see them. Zion could tell that she was especially happy to see him on the street as a free man. She reminded him so much of Laney; it was a shock they weren't really mother and daughter.

She was there with her bodyguard and her new personal assistant, a pretty, little, brown skinned girl that was around Mini's age. They all went out to eat at a restaurant before heading to the Malibu mansion that Mini had been staying in. Zion made it severely clear that he didn't want to be recorded at all, so they had to sit in the truck for thirty minutes while Mini went to go talk to the camera crew about that.

Even with all the cast from the show, the filming crew, and the security team that was staying on the estate, there was still plenty of room for Zion, Laney, and Lester. Zion and Laney shared a room while Lester got his own. Zion was sitting on the bed, watching an interview from his current rival on his phone, when a light knock came on the door.

"Yo!" he answered.

The door opened, and Mini's little pretty ass walked in wearing a pink sundress with a satisfied smile on her face. "Hey, Daddy!"

"Wassup, baby girl?" He returned her greeting with a smile of his own.

"Where's Mommy?" she asked before taking a seat next to him on the bed, her feet dangling off the end of the bed.

He nodded toward the bathroom. "In the shower."

"Okay." She looked down at his phone screen. "That's the man you're supposed to be fighting? I been seeing y'all all over social media."

"Yup, and after I knock his ass out, we going to be twenty-five million dollars richer," he promised.

She released a low whistle. "That's a lot of shopping sprees right there. But on a serious note, can I ask you a favor? You got to promise not to tell Mommy though."

"Of course! Anything for you," he said after placing his phone down on the bed, giving her his undivided attention.

"Well, I might need you to knock this boy out for me. He's my ex, and he's being real sour since I broke up with him."

Zion's eyes hardened. "What he do?" His voice was sterner now.

"Well, he recorded us having sex without me knowing, but I didn't find out until recently when I came out here for the show. He originally extorted me for ten thousand dollars, and I paid it because I thought it was going to be over with after that, but now, he's asking for ten thousand again, and I don't know if he's going to stop. The shit is so stressful because he's really holding that video over a bitch's head on some lame shit... It's bad enough I got OnlyFans content, but I never got fully naked on there. I just dance around in lingerie and tease the men. I get my money off of teasing men. If that video gets out, the value of my brand will go down because men won't have to wonder what I look like naked anymore."

Zion's teeth were clenched, and his heart rate had slightly sped up by the time she was done speaking. "Don't worry about it. I'll handle it, baby girl. You won't have to worry about that video getting out, and you damn sure won't have to worry about paying that lil' nigga another dime. Just send me a picture of him, his address, and his name."

"Thank you soooo much, Zion! I love you!" she assured before placing a quick kiss on his cheek and heading out of the room. "I got a full day planned for us, so tell Mommy to hurry up, so we can get to it."

CHAPTER 25

LANEY

MEANWHILE, IN THE BATHROOM, LANEY SAT NAKED ON THE toilet while the shower water ran. She was enjoying a good shit when her burner phone rang. She initially sighed because it was her work phone, and she informed everyone back home not to bother her unless it was a crisis.

She picked the phone up off the fancy marble floor and looked at the screen. It was a foreign number, and there was only one person she knew outside of the United States. "What the hell you want, J-Rock?"

"Now, that ain't no way to talk to your big homie," he responded evenly. There was no anger in his voice.

Laney rolled her eyes. "What you going to do? Fly back out here and beat me up? I never been scared of you, nigga, and I ain't about to start now. So, like I said, what the hell do you want, J-Rock?"

"Heard you abandoned your post. What's up with that?" The disapproval was evident in his tone, but there still wasn't the usual malice.

"I didn't abandon anything," she assured immediately. "I'm on a short trip to visit Mini. Tory is holding down the fort until I get back. You don't have to keep tabs on me, fool."

"I keep tabs on all my senior staff," he admitted. "Y'all been holding shit down and keeping to the agenda. I like that."

"Of course you do... Is that all?" she asked, not hiding the irritation in her voice.

"Damn, it's like that? Not even going to ask me how it's going out here? How I'm doing?"

She pulled the phone away from her ear and looked at it crazy, as if he could see her, before putting it back to her ear. "It been like that, J-Rock. I'm not going to ask that because I don't care. You made me run your nation, and I'm doing that. If it's not about Rock Nation, we don't have nothing to talk about."

J-Rock chuckled. "Aight, man. As long as you keep doing what you doing, I won't have to kill you and kidnap your daughter. Just remember..."

Laney didn't get to hear what else he had to say because she hung up on his ass and blocked the number. He lost her when he threatened her daughter. He knew how much she cared for Mini and was holding that over her head. Just like that, her anxiety was raised, and her mind was scrambled — exactly what J-Rock's bitch ass wanted to accomplish from his phone call. He wanted to keep her in her place, and just that one fresh threat coming from him was enough to do it.

She placed the phone on the floor and buried her face into her palms. She wanted to kill J-Rock so badly and erase the burden of him away from her life, but he was even more impossible to kill now that he was all the way in Jamaica. But maybe not. There were plenty of Jamaican bosses in America who she could align herself with to help her conspire against him in Jamaica.

What J-Rock didn't know was that she would do *anything* to protect her family, even if it meant attempting to kill his ass again. He would soon find out though, and hopefully, it'd be right before his killer took his evil life.

CHAPTER 26

GLOCK

"I'M ON THE WAY TO THE CHURCH NOW TO MEET THE preacher," Glock told Murk over the phone. "I got this, bruh. I don't need you checking in on the mission."

"I'm not checking in because I don't think you got it. If that was the case, I would've sent some Vultures down there with you. I'm checking in to make sure you straight, lil' nigga," Murk informed seriously.

Glock took a breath. "Yeah, I'm straight, bruh. Everything smooth. Just trying to stay busy so I can keep my mind off of shit."

"I understand, just make sure you keep that temper in check. Never bring emotions on a mission," Murk advised. "Aight, handle yo shit and just keep me posted, fool," he said before ending the call.

Glock was honestly annoyed by Murk's overbearingness, but by now, he could tell Murk had his best interest for real, so he started accepting Murk's counsel more and more over the weeks. He wasn't used to taking orders from another man, but he was learning a lot from Murk, so he fell in line. It was a smart move for himself and his gang.

They arrived at a huge church that surprised Glock with its beauty. "This muthafucka nicer than I expected."

"Yeah, all the Black people in the county come to this church. It ain't nothing but a fashion show. Like a high school," Dang informed from the backseat.

Glock glanced back at him through the rearview mirror. "This better not be a setup, or we going to pay yo' grandmother a visit at that facility."

"Man, that's a real church service going on in there. Pastor Mack don't play. He run his congregation like a military unit. Nigga like a drill sergeant for God or some shit," Dang explained to the best of his ability.

Ruga's face crumbled. "What kind of shit is that?"

"Just how it is. He got some questionable methods as a pastor, but that nigga done did a lot of good throughout my lifetime."

Glock nodded. "Ruga, find a parking spot. We going to kick it out here until the end of the service," Glock instructed, ready to meet Pastor Mack. He wanted to see how he would deal with Rock Nation on his doorstep.

———

The service lasted for about another hour before churchgoers began to exit the building, so they could head home. Glock and his gang hopped out of their vehicles after over half of the parked cars pulled out of the lot twenty minutes later.

Dang led them into the church right through the front

entrance. A small group of young women stood just outside of the church, and one caught Glock's eye in a unique way. She stood out from the other two females easily, and she was looking dead at him with her sexy, mischievous eyes and puffed up, curly hair.

Her light skin matched her yellow-brown hair, and while all that was cool, it was her perfectly sculpted body that was doing it for him. She had thighs and the right amount of stomach. She was a chubby goddess, and Glock couldn't help him damn self. He had always seen himself as the catch and didn't usually approach women first, but he was walking in her direction before he knew it.

"Now you know you wearing that muthafuckin' dress if you got me pulling up, approaching you in front of a church, on some thirsty shit," Glock stated as a form of greeting. All three women wore dresses, but it was clear who he was talking to because his stare burned into her eyes as he neared.

He had on black Air Forces, skinny, black jeans with rips in them, and a black Armani hoodie on over a black t-shirt. The only piece of jewelry he had on were his solitary diamond earrings that couldn't be seen until he pulled the hoodie off of his head. His box braids were stuffed inside of his hoodie too, so they were revealed as well.

"Yeah, this one arrogant ass bastard right here. If he pulling up on you, you got to be special. I'm not even going to lie," Ruga cosigned truthfully.

It was clear that the females were a little intimidated by their strong approach. They stood there like deer in head-lights, so Glock softened his approach. "What's your name, Fluffy?"

"Looks like you already gave me a name," she replied through a slight blush. He could notice her struggling to keep her composure.

Glock had her right where he wanted her. He was about to go in for the kill when he heard Dang. "Pastor Mack!"

Glock watched in surprise as Pastor Mack stepped out of the church. Dang forgot to mention that he was 6'6" with a linebacker's build. All eyes were on him as he approached.

"I see you've met my daughter, Kelsey, and her friends," Pastor Mack observed while eyeing Glock and his men.

"Your grown daughter, right?" Glock asked hopefully while taking a step up toward the pastor.

Pastor Mack locked eyes with Glock and slowly nodded his head up and down. "She's over twenty-one but also the most precious thing in my life, so I'd tread lightly, young man."

"Well, obviously you don't know me too well," Glock challenged fearlessly. He never cared about the size of the man because anyone could be brought down with a bullet. "I came to talk business though. I'll catch up with you on my own time," he told Kelsey before making his way past the pastor, into the church, with his men in tow.

"This muthafucka look like one of them churches that be on TV," Glock complimented as he looked around at the high ceilings on the inside.

"Watch your language in this house of worship," Pastor Mack commanded sternly after walking in behind them.

Glock licked his lips before displaying a nasty sneer. He turned toward the pastor and locked eyes with him. "Take a good look into my eyes and see if you see fear, nigga. God is for the fearing man, and that's not me. I worship myself so miss me with that religious shit. I'm not here to talk to the pastor of the church. I'm here to talk to the ringleader of Choppa Family, and all hands point to you."

The pastor clenched his teeth and took a deep breath. "Follow me."

They followed the pastor into his personal office where he fixed himself a drink of wine then took a seat behind his desk. "So, you're Rock Nation coming to extort me, correct?"

"I mean, if that's how you want to look at it. It's really more of a business deal but can turn into straight up extortion if we don't close that deal."

The pastor nodded his understanding before taking another sip from his cup. "Well, you should've did your homework before you came all this way, youngin. This is a white town, and we're just living in it. I pay dues to the crackers on the other side of town to keep a leash on those crazy ass Aryans."

"Wait, wait, wait!" Glock shouted. "So, you mean to tell me you already getting extorted by some fucking crackers? And you a tax paying citizen? So, you really getting it up the ass two ways. That's some real slave shit."

Ruga and the rest of his men were laughing by the time he was finished. Glock said what came to his mind and didn't apologize for his bluntness.

"Call it what you want, but it's kept my people safe for all this time. I'm responsible for my people, and I make the necessary sacrifices needed for our survival. I'm all they've got."

Glock shook his head. "That ain't no way to live, big dawg. Me just being who I am, at this point, this shit just turned personal."

"Awww, shit. My boy, *Harriet Glockman,* about to free the slaves," Ruga chimed in, barely able to contain his own laughter.

Pastor Mack shook his head. "Listen. Just go back to Charlotte and tell your boss that it's a lose-lose situation. Those white men that's pulling the strings is the mayor, judges, and sheriffs. This a fight even Rock Nation can't win."

"It's obvious you got basic knowledge on Rock Nation. I like that you not lost in the sauce, but what you need to do is call up to Charlotte and ask about Glock Gang. You'll learn that we do well against all odds. Just keep doing what you doing and I'll handle the rest," Glock instructed before standing up from his seat and exiting the pastor's office. "Send for ten Glocks. No safety," he commanded Ruga. It was code, meaning to call for ten shooters that were ready to shoot without any hesitation whatsoever.

Ruga hopped on his phone as they exited the church, and Glock looked around to see if Kelsey was still around. "One of y'all remind me to catch up with that nigga's daughter too. I need that," he said seriously.

CHAPTER 27

ICE

ICE WAS AT ONE OF HIS CONDOS, RUNNING HIS MONEY through a money counter. He was nearing a hundred thousand for a week's work. His crew was so efficient and responsible, so his hands weren't full at all. His main focuses these days had been keeping up with —_and investing —_the money. Shit had been smooth for him up until he bumped heads with Big Body a few months back.

He was still mad about his two thieving ass soldiers. They had gotten caught with their hands in the wrong cookie jar, and Ice made sure they were dealt with properly. Big Body probably felt like they should've been spared, so he was obviously taking it out on Ice. Ice was fed up with Big Body, who'd crossed the line. They were eternal enemies now.

"Look. I just reached a hundred thousand and still got more bills to run through the counter. I get a load like this every Monday from my crew. I have an entire empire at my disposal, but right now, it's in need of protection. As the king, it's up to me to protect what's mines, and that's why I'm standing in front of y'all now, trying to figure out if y'all the right men for the job," Ice informed with a raised brow.

He was interviewing a military lieutenant and a few members of his unit. They were all deployed from active duty and doing what they could do to get by in America's harsh society. Ice did his research on them and was offering them a real career, making retirement money.

"Okay. Now that we're face-to-face, I'm going to need you to keep it straight with me. I reviewed the salaries and benefits you're offering to us, and if I'm honest, it raises some questions. Before we commit to the job, I need to know exactly what I'm getting my men into," Lieutenant Jackson informed seriously. He was a well-built, Black man with a low service cut and a big beard. He sounded just as intimidating as he looked.

Lieutenant Jackson had three other men from his unit with him — one white man, a Hispanic, and another Black man. They probably all came from different backgrounds and experienced different shit, but it was clear that they had been through some shit together as well. They shared body language and energy. They moved as one, like Murk and his Vultures. Ice took positive note of that.

"Honestly, the less you know, the better," Ice answered straightly. "It's simple. I want the same loyalty, respect, and commitment that you gave the military. And y'all shouldn't have a problem with that because, unlike the government, I take very *good* care of mines."

Lieutenant Jackson's men looked at him, awaiting his response. LT stood up out of his chair, to his full six-foot height, and closed the distance between himself and Ice. "That's some real shit you just spit, but I think I get the picture. Let me huddle with my men, and I'll be back in touch with a final decision no later than tomorrow night," he said with a firm hand extended for a good shake.

———

After counting his money, Ice threw it back inside of the MCM bag it came in and left the condo. He rarely used that spot. He bought it for one of his girlfriends a few years ago, but he'd recently evicted her from his life, so he was still figuring out what to do with the place. It was a perfect meeting spot for today's interview though.

He had high hopes, big plans, and big responsibilities for Lieutenant Jackson. He was the missing piece to Ice's puzzle, so Ice was on edge. He needed LT to accept the job because he was in dire need of security. He was a dolphin in the same tank as whales and sharks. Recent events showed his vulnerabilities, and like any smart man, he sought out to harden them. If LT accepted the job, he'd just throw in the condo as a bonus. Fuck it.

He cruised smoothly through the busy Charlotte afternoon traffic, listening to Lil Wayne's *No Ceilings*. It was one of his favorite mixtapes of all time and meditation music for him these days. A few minutes later, he was pulling up to one of Charlotte's newest fun houses. It was Ice's business, and he was already making huge profits from a two-year-old investment.

Ice Cold Fun Town had recently become a hotspot in

the city for family fun. There was a giant arcade, bowling alley, go cart racing, and even a paintball shooting course. People of all ages came to the Fun House for fun. He had a whole food court in there and all. He spared no expense when renovating the place, and it turned out to be one of his greatest accomplishments and investments toward his empire — something legit to pass down to his children. A real legacy, and it was just the beginning.

He parked his AMG Benz in his reserved parking space and hopped out with the MCM bookbag in hand. It was three o'clock on a Tuesday afternoon, and the place was already jumping. They were open Monday through Sunday from noon to midnight, and customers took full advantage of the opening hours. The place was a goldmine. His staff was even turnt up, making more money than the average nine-to-five workers in the city.

As soon as you walked into the Fun House, you were in the food court. It was the first thing you saw, right before the oversized arcade. He didn't know he was hungry until all the tasty food smells assaulted his nostrils. He decided he had a taste for a Chinese plate, so he got in line and purchased a shrimp fried rice and fried chicken meal to go. He could've pulled his VIP card as the owner, but he was feeling extra humble on that particular day.

After receiving his food, Ice made his way into one of the restricted areas of the building. There was a restricted area for the staff employees, and there was a restricted area for his crew. They called themselves M.I.A., which stood for *Money Intelligence Agency*. They were easily some of the most respected scammers on the East Coast. There were major scam crews in New York City that weren't even fucking with them in real life. Ice just made sure his people stayed humble and lowkey. It was their secret to success, the only reason they'd made it that far without getting caught up in a Fed sweep.

He walked down two flights of stairs that led to one single, thick, steel plated door. Ice pulled out his phone and opened an app that scanned his face and opened the door. He walked into the M.I.A. headquarters, feeling like he was at home. They called it the Federal Reserve. It was their own exclusive mini fun house.

It was set up like an upscale club, but to them, it was just an underground mansion. "What y'all in here cooking up? I hope y'all made some progress from yesterday," said Ice as he walked into the glass conference room.

Two of his students were hostages in the Federal Reserve until they drew up five legitimate business plans for the agency. Yasmine and Big Money had both been working for him for a year now but had only met him two weeks ago when he got word of their latest scheme.

Yasmine and Big Money were middle school sweethearts. They clicked when they were both thirteen and were still joined at the hip a whole twenty years later. They started off pulling small scams with bad checks; now they were in the major league. Their latest stunt had put them on another level and Ice's radar.

Ice noticed their true ambition after they cloned thousands of Amazon gift cards in a single week. It took less time than that to receive and resell the delivered products. Even while reselling the products at half price, they still made off with a little over a million dollars, even after paying their dues to M.I.A. That was definitely the type of dedication he needed on his legal team.

"We're done," Yasmine informed matter-of-factly. "We're thinking about slogans and shit now."

Ice nodded his approval with a half-smile. "Y'all emailed me the business plans?"

Yasmine and Big Money nodded in unison.

"Aight. Porsha here?" he asked.

"She's in the lab," Yasmine answered.

Ice dipped out of the conference room and made his way toward the lab. Most of his crew was too busy to lounge around the Federal Reserve like Ice and Porsha. Porsha was Ice's first love and partner-in-crime. She helped him build his empire. It was just as much hers as it was his.

Porsha wasn't pale white like Ice, but she had the brightest yellow skin. Her long, curly, sandy brown hair and hazel eyes were her best features since she didn't have a curvy body. She was flat up top and down low. Ice didn't give a fuck though. He loved her inside and out.

"What you in here working on, little girl?" he asked as he walked into the lab.

The lab was a fully digitized room filled with some of the latest tech the world had to offer. There were holographic computers and tablets. The chalkboard was even holographic. There wasn't a pen or paper in sight. It was where the major bucks were made. Porsha graduated to hacking about six years ago, and she was a big deal these days in that field.

"I'm not working right this second. I'm playing this game designed by this master hacker guy. But it's some real-life shit because the characters in the game are hackers, so you basically learning while you playing. I paid 40K for the program, and it's just now finally uploading, so yeah... This is what I'm on for the day," she informed with satisfaction, letting him know to give her some space.

She stood up in front of a large monitor with a homemade controller in her hand. She only had on tights with a sports bra, just how he liked her. He walked up behind her and wrapped his arms around her as he buried his face in her neck. "You can play this shit in our room. Come kick it with a nigga."

"Fuck no! You going to distract me. I need to stay focused right now. I'm working on something big, and this game is going to help me accomplish that," she answered seriously.

"Trying to land our ass in the Feds," he joked.

She quickly paused the game, broke away from his grasp, and spun around toward him in the same motion. "Now, why the hell would you say that, Israel? Why?"

"I'm just saying, bae... How much more you trying to accomplish? After you pulled that last lil' stunt, I just knew you would be on cruise control, now you trying to go harder?" he asked, referring to the last digital heist she'd committed a few months ago.

Porsha swiped nine million from a major corporation like it was nothing. It was the perfect heist because the pharmaceutical company couldn't report it since it was money that they weren't legally supposed to have in the first place. So, Ice was genuinely curious as to why she still had the same hunger she did when they were still petty hustling.

"Yes! You damn right I'm trying to go harder. I'm

looking at the bigger picture, Ice! The world is going to shit, and I'm just making moves to ensure that our family will be royal when it's all said and done... Speaking of moves, how was your meeting with the security team?"

Ice nodded his head, licked his lips, and rubbed his hands, all at the same time, while looking at her with satisfaction. "I got a good feeling about them guys. I can smell the death on them, and more importantly, I sense loyalty amongst them. They solid, and I know they going to be the perfect fit within our organization."

"Okay, good." She smiled a smile of relief. "They're just the tip of the iceberg though. We need an army of our own because it's obvious Rock Nation won't protect us."

"I told Lieutenant Jackson all that good shit. I just got to chop it up with him a lil' bit more, and we all set. I know he going to make the right decision."

She turned back toward the monitor and un-paused the game. "Alright... I'll see you later on. Let me focus. I won't be able to get shit done with you in here."

"Fuck that raggedy ass game!" he spat jokingly as he made his way out of the lab.

He gave her a hard time mostly, but she was one of the most precious things on Earth to him. He was lucky to have such a strong and smart woman on his side for all these years. He had to protect her —_and his family —_by all means.

CHAPTER 28

GLOCK

GLOCK DIDN'T WANT TO SLEEP IN THE INFESTED MOTEL, SO he took up residency inside of Dang's house. Of course, Dang didn't oppose, but Glock could tell he didn't want them staying in his home. Glock, being Glock, assured Dang that this takeover wouldn't take long, and they'd be out of his way in no time.

Like always, he had confidence in himself, his gang, and their abilities, but he was still a little weary about the task ahead. If Pastor Mack was correct, then he would have to really think this out, especially when dealing with white people. They played by different rules, and if they had judges and politicians in their pocket, then that meant the entire city belonged to them. That included the sheriff and prosecutor.

He sat up on the upstairs hallway floor with his back against the wall, smoking a cigarette. He was restless and needed to be proactive, so he jumped into drill-sergeant-mode. He snatched the hood from over his head as he stood up to his feet and made his way to Dang's room. Dang was out cold, sleeping like a baby.

"Get yo' ass up, bruh! We got shit to accomplish. Ain't no time for sleep. Meet me downstairs," Glock shouted forcefully, tearing Dang from a deep sleep.

"What time is it?" asked Dang after looking over at the window and not seeing any sunshine.

"It's four o'clock, nigga! Get the fuck up!" he spat. "I know you want us up out yo' shit. Bring your ass down-stairs and help."

A few short minutes later, Glock had the whole house wide awake and gathered together in the living room. "Alright, I got ten more Glocks on the way, but that's just manpower. What we need to stick it to these white folks is a solid ass plan. And not just any plan either. We need a real-deal plan."

"What you got in mind so far?" one of his main Glocks asked curiously.

"Well, from what I was told by the pastor after the meeting, them folks run a real tight ship. They got a mean structure, and they high on security, so it's definitely going to be a sticky situation. Not gone be easy at all," Glock evaluated honestly.

"Shit's a damn suicide mission, for the tenth time!" Dang stated in deep frustration. "Those honkeys are mili-tant as fuck. Just leave shit how it is out here. This is their town. Let them have it because this doesn't end well for us."

Glock nodded his understanding. "I respect what you saying because I thought about the shit myself at first, but this shit deeper than what you think. My superiors hold me to a high standard for a reason, so failure ain't an option for real. Plus, this a righteous cause. Got to see this shit through. Can't fold. My kind, we just don't fold, gang. So, like I said, we need a solid plan, nigga."

"You gone have to lock arms with the pastor on that note. He been dealing with them crackers for over a decade. He knows all about them," said Dang before taking a deep breath and standing up. "I'm going back to sleep."

Ruga and two of the other Glocks popped up out of their seats and blocked Dang's way as he tried to head back upstairs. "You don't leave the table until you dismissed!" Ruga spat.

Glock released a light laugh. "Nah, let him go upstairs. He need to get some rest because he got to go find the pastor's daughter and bring her to me later on. She can come with her friends if they with her."

Dang snapped his head back at Glock. "You going after the pastor's daughter ain't going to work, my nigga. You want to be friends with the pastor, not his enemy."

"That bitch grown. I'm not trying to hear all that shit," Glock spat. "She got a part to play in all this as well."

When Dang was upstairs and out of sight, they returned to their spots in the living room.

"Ruga, when the other Glocks get here, I want you to take them to that apartment complex and secure them some apartments. We about to set up shop out this bitch," said Glock before pulling the hoodie back over his head and taking a seat on one of the couches.

"So, how long you think this whole mission going to take?" Mark asked curiously. "You know I got two bitches back in the city, and one of them pregnant. Can't be away for too long." He was one of Glock Gang's most feared enforcers.

"Tell them you'll be gone at least a month. About to be doing monthly rotations on deployment. We're here to expand Rock Nation, but I figure why not expand Glock Gang in the process... Don't trip though. I'm not gone crash us out. I'm gone do it big for Ja'Kiyah."

CHAPTER 29
LANEY

LANEY PEEPED MINI'S WHOLE SCENE OUT OVER THE weekend, and she loved what she saw. Mini was killing it, and she shined so much brighter than most of the girls there. The only other girl that was on Mini's level was the only white girl on the show, and she was now Mini's new best friend, so the rest of the girls naturally hated on them, but they couldn't be stopped.

They were different but had a weird and cute bond that the pubic obviously loved because they were already going viral on social media for their online documentary show, *Days in the Life of Mini & Kate*. They livestreamed that during the filming of the main show, so it was a two-way promotional machine and automatically made them the faces of the upcoming urban series.

The show's host, Deanna Vallahngssbi, was easily one of the prettiest bitches in the world. Laney had done her homework on her and couldn't even downplay it. Deanna was doing her damn thing. Her husband came from generations of wealth, and she didn't have to lift another finger in this lifetime, but she still went hard on her grind. Laney respected that and was sure her husband did as well.

She patiently waited for Deanna to wrap up an important conversation with one of the producers. They were in the backyard shooting a scene where the girls planned the big party that they were throwing at the house. It was a competition to see who could get the most people to attend. It was invitation only, and each digital pass let you know which girl it came from.

"You know my baby's going to win this little contest right here," said Laney once Deanna had walked back over to where she stood. "I'm not taking nothing from the rest of these girls but come on now."

Deanna nodded her head believably. "I'm sure every one of these girl's mothers would tell me the same thing, but that's just in our nature. It's the unmatched love that we have for our children that cause us to believe that, but I can tell that you're saying it because you know what Mini's capable of. After studying her and spending this time around Mini, I can tell she is a powerful force, but she still has a lot to learn about the industry before she jumps in."

Laney looked over at Mini, who mingled around her peers. She was in a cute bikini with a linen halter top. Her big sunglasses intensified her bossy personality. Mini was putting on a show for the camera and knew exactly what she was doing. She was making her mark in the reality TV industry. "That's exactly why I want you to take those two up under your wing after this show. There's big money to be made, and you know it. Especially with the little white girl. That's the best of both worlds right there."

Deanna laughed. "You're one helluva bitch, girl. I'm convinced you can sell sand to a beach owner."

Laney shrugged. "I'm a woman of vision, and when I'm locked in, I go hard to make it a reality."

"I see where Mini gets it from because that little girl is going places."

"Periodt!" Laney strongly agreed with much enthusiasm. "And we're going to be her GPS system along the way. I promise you won't regret it."

———

After the backyard scene, the girls left to do a beach scene in Malibu, so Laney turned her focus onto her king. Zion was in their room, sitting on the edge of their bed, watching a movie on the TV while eating sunflower seeds.

"The girls went to the beach. I wasn't about to do all that," she informed as she crawled into the bed behind him. "What you in here watching, boy?"

"One of these damn *Fast and Furious'*. I done lost count of them by now," he answered before looking back to face her. "Why you ain't want to go to the beach? What's wrong with you?"

Laney shrugged. "Just wasn't feeling it. Rather be in here with my man."

He grabbed his sunflower seeds and the plastic bag he was spitting them into and scooted back onto the bed with her. "Like I told you while I was locked up, shawty, you can be all up on a nigga as much as you want. I don't mind having you in my skin because I'm in love with yo' choco-late ass."

Laney digested his words with a smile as she cozied up next to his hard body. "Good, nigga. We fly back home tomorrow. I wish we could stay out here for a little while longer. It's so damn peaceful."

"After I win this fight, we're going to take a lot more peaceful trips like this," he promised before kissing her on the forehead.

She gave him a knowing look. "Bae, you know good and damn well J-Rock ain't going for that. That nigga evil and spiteful. That ain't no good mixture. Sorry to tell you, bae, but ain't no way out this shit for me. Unless I get his ass killed somehow."

He didn't respond, and Laney didn't say another word either. She really started to feel bad on the inside. She would forever be tied to the streets with the threat of losing her freedom. Zion had just escaped those walls and had gone fully legit. She didn't want to hold him down. She finally knew what he used to mean when he used to tell her the same thing while he was gone. Just that fast, she had turned into the burden.

She wrapped her arms around him, and he held her securely. She was unconscious before she knew it.

CHAPTER 30
TORY

TORY WAS AT ONE OF THE STASH SPOTS, SECURING A LOAD of cash from last week, when he got a call from Careesha. "Bitch, you better not be into no bullshit!" he barked upon answering. He had given her very specific instructions to stay lowkey before sending her back to the country.

"I'm not into nothing. Wasn't nothing for me back in my hometown, so I took my crew with me," she informed smugly.

"Where the fuck you at?" he asked with a raised brow.

"Just rented a big ass house out here in Charlotte. On your side of town to be exact."

Tory paused before walking away from the kitchen table. Choppa kept counting.

"Bruh, you know you supposed to check-in before doing shit like that. You gone make Laney feel like you trying to play mind games, and that's not what you want, baby girl. You got to watch how you move these days," he stressed seriously.

Careesha had miles of potential. She was just hard-headed, and that could get her ass killed when operating at that level of the game. There wasn't too much room for disorder.

"Ain't nobody trying to play mind games. I'm a whole asset to the nation. I'm here to kiss Laney's ring, nigga. I want more for me and mines. Too big for that little ass town we're from," she stated sincerely.

He could hear it in her voice. "Man, send me the address. I'm gone head there after I finish my routes for the day," he instructed before ending the call.

———

Tory kept his word and made time for Careesha. He actually had some personal business he needed to handle before he ended the night, but he obviously had a soft spot for the bitch. Her little pretty ass did something to him. She was sweet and soft on the outside and iron and steel on the inside — a true gutter bitch from the dirt. Definitely his type of bitch.

"Bitch definitely got a big ass house," he said to Choppa once they pulled up to the address.

"Yeah, she picked a good ass neighborhood too. I figured it had to be out here when you told me a big ass house on the west side. Ain't too many big, big houses on our side like that," said Choppa while looking up at the house as they pulled up the driveway.

Two Mercedes Benz E-class cars and a big U-Haul truck sat in the driveway. "This bitch wasn't playing. She dead serious tired of that country life."

They got out of the Lamborghini Urus and headed to the front door. Careesha answered the door in a black spandex bodysuit and furry slippers to match. "How you like my shit?"

"This ain't yo' shit, but it's hard though."

She rolled her eyes. "Fuck you, nigga. I'm renting to own," she informed matter-of-factly.

"Ain't nothing wrong with that... How many bodies you brought with you?" he stated then asked after watching a man walk past inside of the house.

She stepped aside, so they could come inside and get out of the cold. "Three bitches and two of their niggas. All of them works for me. My main crew so I brought they ass with me."

They followed her into the living room where boxes were stacked up. A lady and a man went through them and sorted through stuff. "So, you really setting up shop out here, huh?" he asked her seriously.

Careesha stood there and nodded her head defiantly. "Hell yeah. We only get one life, and I plan on doing it big with mines. My crew feel the exact same. We ready to put in the work, Tory."

"I understand that, and I respect that shit, but I'm going to need y'all to sit down somewhere until I can figure out a place for y'all in the organization."

She gave him an obvious look. "Right up under you, nigga! I know you need help running this hectic ass ship. Y'all doing numbersssss. I know you can use some trust-worthy hands to help you keep it afloat."

"I'll get back with you in a few days. For now, focus on

furnishing this pretty ass house," he advised while taking another good look at the interior design.

"Furniture getting delivered first thing in the morning, nigga. Don't try me! Don't forget about a bitch!" she barked as he walked off.

He looked back with a knowing face. "How could I ever forget about yo' lil' fine ass?" he asked before letting himself out of the house.

CHAPTER 31

MURK

"WHY WE GOT TO COME WITH THESE NIGGAS? THEY GOT the whole BBG at their disposal," Swiss asked out of genuine curiosity. There was nothing normal about this exchange.

"This ain't no normal circumstances," Murk reminded. "Tell the guys to watch these niggas. Just because they being sent by J-Rock, we don't know these folks," he said before walking away from the car window and over to Tory's car window.

They were on the back streets in Tory's neighborhood, parked in a cul-de-sac where they were about to meet the Jamaican rastas that J-Rock had sent to supply them with guns. They were friends of J-Rock's cousin, but Tory didn't trust it, so he called up Murk just in case shit got real ugly. Murk knew Tory would put his pride to the side when it came to certain shit, and tonight was a perfect example.

"These niggas running late, and it's starting to rain. They got ten more minutes, and we relocating the drop spot. Fuck they thought?" he said after Tory rolled down his window.

Tory nodded his head as Black 'N' Mild smoke escaped his big nostrils. "Say less. They need to come through though. We need this shipment. We ain't had a big shipment of guns in a while."

"We got more soldiers to equip now, so it make sense," Murk responded while looking down the road for the truck. "Ten more minutes, like I said. We pulling off after that," he reminded before heading back into his truck.

"What that nigga talking about?" asked Swiss curiously.

"Not shit," he answered flatly. "I'm more worried about Glock out there on that mission, bruh."

Swiss chuckled. "I would be worried too, nigga. That lil' nigga is a fucking ticking time bomb with a crew of suicidal lil' niggas ready to crash out right behind his ass."

"Shit, that's how we started until we got right. That lil' nigga got more sense than he let folks believe. He gone handle it. Watch."

Murk rolled a Backwood filled with exotic weed and sparked it while they waited for the Jamaicans.

CHAPTER 32
GLOCK

THE NEXT MORNING, WHILE RUGA GOT THE GUYS SITUATED in the apartments, Glock grilled some burgers on Dang's back patio like it was his own. It was kind of warm for a day in March, so Glock figured he'd crank the grill up. Why not?

He had music blasting from his phone speaker, so he barely heard Dang coming through the back sliding door of the house. He grabbed his pistol off the side of the grill with cat like speed and trained it on Dang with his free hand before he could step all the way onto the patio.

"Woahhhh! It's just me, man. I'm back with the package," he informed with both hands up high before stepping all the way onto the patio, so Kelsey could follow.

Glock immediately placed the gun back onto the side of the grill. "Oh, look who done made it," he said with much enthusiasm.

Dang had been gone for a while, trying to locate and grab her, but Glock was prepared for her arrival. He had on some skinny, black, designer jeans, black, shiny Pradas on his feet, and a simple, black, Ralph Lauren t-shirt that fit him snugly. His braids were down, and he was bad bitch ready. Black designer clothes and black guns to match. He felt like fucking Batman sometimes.

"I'm surprised she came by herself. I just knew she was going to bring her lil' friends with her," he thought aloud.

Kelsey smiled a seriously adorable smile. "I definitely tried to get them to come, but they were too scared."

"So, what made you came? You not scared?" he asked after walking around the grill and closing the distance between them.

She looked up at him, only two feet away from her now. "I'm not going to say that I'm not, but my curiosity is overriding that. Obviously overriding my common sense. I'm sure my friends already sent word to my father that I'm with the boy he warmed me about the other night."

"Warned you about?" he asked with a smile. "What did he say about me?"

"That you're the worst type of person and I need to stay *farrr* away from you," she answered truthfully. He could tell she was telling the whole truth just then.

"Well, guess what... your daddy was right. I am the worst type of person to most people, but that don't mean I'll be a bad person to you."

She didn't respond, just blushed slightly as she averted eye contact, so he continued. "And don't worry about your father. We'll handle him. Ain't that right, Dang?"

Dang pressed his lips together and nodded his head with wide eyes. His expression drew laughter from Glock. Dang was a funny ass nigga on the low.

G lock cooked enough for Kelsey, Dang, and himself, but only Kelsey ate on the back patio with him at the table. She had loosened up over the hour she'd been there, and they had covered some ground.

"My best friend, Alexis, stays over there, and her father is the sheriff. I think I can convince her to get her father to see things your way. They share that type of relationship," Kelsey informed matter-of-factly, like she had all the answers to his current problems.

She surprised him with her willingness to help the cause. He broke down the entire predicament to her, and to his surprise, she knew all about it. She was way more knowledgeable than her father would ever imagine. Apparently, the sheriff told his daughter everything, and she poured Kelsey all the tea when she was drunk. Kelsey didn't drink too much, so she remembered *everything* her bestie had told her over all the years.

"Look at God," said Glock. He had a feeling she would play apart in his success out there. "So, you think you can get a meeting arranged?"

Kelsey shrugged. "I'll have to see about that."

"Tell him I got him ten thousand just to sit down and talk to me. We can meet in Walmart if he want, but the only way I'm doing business is face-to-face."

"Damn," she spat. "You're serious about this, I see."

"Hell yeah, man. God landed me right here at this specific point in my life for a reason. I already made up my mind. I'm setting up shop out here, and I'm gone change this town for the better. This my first year on campus, and I'm about to go punch the bully in the face."

Kelsey gave him a satisfied stare. "And that's exactly why I'm helping you. Not because you're handsome but because you have strong, good energy, and you have good intentions. You're about to stick your neck out for my people, so you have my trust and respect."

"That's real." He was feeling her personality and mindset. Pastor Mack had obviously raised her right. "Only if yo' damn daddy had that same energy. He rather be a slave."

Kelsey looked at him. "He means well, and he does a lot for our people. He just doesn't see life through your eyes, so you two have different approaches."

"I like you, bruh. You smart, and you say what's on your mind... I'm not even gon' lie. I initially wanted to seduce you, so I could fuck you, but I see so much potential in you for real. Got a strong feeling that I need to keep you close. Like I'm ready to hire you on spot."

"Hire me as what?" she asked as she allowed herself to blush.

"An assistant."

"I don't know. I can't be around all these guns and drugs like that... I have a bright future. I can't risk that."

Glock laughed. "You don't have to ride around with us or nothing like that. We can talk over the phone most times. The only time I'm going to need to see you in person is when I take you on dates and shit," he finished with a sinister smirk.

She couldn't help but to smirk back.

CHAPTER 33
LANEY

As soon as they were back in town, Zion shot to the gym. He had to put in extra work to make up for his lazy days. Laney's shit had been run smoothly while she was gone, so she didn't have to scramble once she was back. She missed her home, so she spent her first day back in her home. She literally had a dream home now, and she had to get *real* aquatinted with the place. She had a million plans for the place already. She was about to act bad on the decorations.

She was in the basement, looking around. It had a unique layout and a lot of potential, but she ultimately decided to leave it alone. She would leave that section alone for Zion. It would be his sanctuary.

She headed back upstairs and played with the little Yorkie puppies that Zion bought her — one boy and one girl.

Thoughts of her vacation were fresh in her head, and she suddenly remembered the disturbing phone call she got from J-Rock's bitch ass. He had threatened her daughter one too many times, so there she was once again, plotting on the best way to end his evil life and send him back to hell.

She hated that she had to go to those extremes, but she would do *anything* to protect her loved ones. She made up her mind right then that she would talk to Karmen about the whole ordeal soon. She had to take another shot at his ass.

"It better not be no damn bullshit either," she spat as her business phone vibrated on the floor. She picked it up. It was Tory. "Wassup, nigga?"

"How was the trip?"

"Let's just say that Cali owes me nothing... Heard shit been smooth out this way while I been gone. It need to stay that damn way for a while. I don't got the energy for that mess right now."

"Don't even trip. Kick your feet up. Let me keep doing what I been doing. I got all the bases covered," he assured seriously.

Laney looked at her phone and shrugged her shoulders. If Tory wanted to be the class pet, she would let him. She needed all the free time she could get, so she could plan her exit. She refused to let J-Rock win. The game wasn't over.

"Alright, but make sure you come to me about the serious shit though. Don't just go to making big decisions now," she warned sternly.

"You know I got you, Boss Lady," he promised. "Well, this isn't that important but worth you knowing." He told her all about Careesha moving her crew to Charlotte and requesting to work under him.

"Nah, she need to get her ass back down there. We got money coming out of her town."

"She say she already got all of that under control. She got a replacement down there, and the money's going to still flow."

Laney picked up one of the dogs with her free hand and raised it eye level with her. "I guess. Keep a tight leash on that bitch though. I wouldn't trust her as far as I can throw her."

"Copy that," said Tory before ending the call.

Laney placed the phone on the hardwood floor and picked up the other dog. She was in deep thought, trying to map out the best version of her near future. The rest of her day would consist of deep thinking and deep cleaning. It was her therapy.

CHAPTER 34
ZION

Zion had an important stop to make before he submerged himself in the gym. He'd been so busy and focused since he'd been out of prison that he didn't really have time for side-quests yet. This was important business though and needed to be handled by him immediately.

His driver zipped him to the westside where he met up with Big Body at a house around the way. This was only Zion's third time back in his old neighborhood since his release. He'd been so busy training and bonding with his loved ones to do anything else. He was on a mission.

"You ain't have to come out here, bruh. This shit was handled," Big Body said as Zion hopped out of the SUV with a fitted black Nike sweatsuit.

He looked at Big Body with a nasty mug. "I don't wanna hear that shit, nigga. This personal business right here," he spat before leading the way into the house.

There were a few unfamiliar faces inside of the house, but he didn't see who he was there for. "Where he at?"

"In the basement, fool. We don't leave hostages in da living room," said Big Body before leading the way to the basement.

Zion pulled his ski mask over his head as they neared the bottom of the basement stairs. Mini's little boyfriend was tied up in a corner of the unfinished basement. It was a pathetic sight — scrawny, little, light skinned kid balled up in a basement. "Get your bitch ass up!"

The little nigga looked up with tears in his eyes. "I was going to give her back the money. I swear!"

"He been singing that same tune since we snatched his lil' ass up," Big Body informed. "He already knew what we was there for. He know he had fucked up."

"Untie him," Zion instructed.

Big Body pulled out a switchblade and cut the zip tie on the lil' nigga's ankles and wrists. He rolled over to where he was sitting up on his ass, looking up at Zion.

"Stand up, lil' nigga. What's your name?" Zion commanded then asked firmly.

"Christian," he said after he was fully on his feet. The young nigga was clearly terrified.

Zion shook his head in disappointment. The lil' nigga looked so damn pitiful that it almost saved him, but Zion wasn't going to let him off the hook that easily. "Put yo shit up, nigga. We about to get us one in!" he commanded after squaring up.

It was clear that Christian really wasn't about that gangster life, but it was also clear that he wasn't a fighter either. He stood there, looking like a tall and scrawny praying mantis, holding up his fighting stance.

Zion heard Big Body grimace as he approached Christian with his own fighting stance in the air. He didn't want to kill the lil' nigga, but he had to learn a lesson. Extortion was serious business, and he needed to know that it wasn't okay.

"Don't ever threaten Mini in any type of way ever again," he commanded before reflecting one of Christian's punches and landing a crucial blow to his stomach.

Christian immediately dropped to the ground and curled up in pain. "Aghhhhh!" he cried out once he had caught some breath.

"Get yo' lil' bitch ass up, nigga. Want to extort my muthafuckin' people like this shit something to be played with," Zion spat.

Big Body's hand shot up to cover his nose. "Oh, nooo! I think this lil' nigga done shitted on himself. I can smell it, bruh!"

Zion looked from Big Body to Christian and took a deep breath of the air. Big Body was definitely right. The stench was faint at the moment, but he knew fresh shit when he smelled it.

"I'm not even going to touch you no more. I think you get the picture at this point," said Zion as he approached Christian once again, but his fighting guard wasn't up this time.

He kneeled down, so he could get closer to Christian. The stench of shit was much stronger than it was across the room. "Stay away from Mini, bruh. Block her on social media, block her number, and I *better not* hear of you around her again. You will return that money, and you going to owe her that same amount. You getting off light right now though, so thank whatever God you pray to because your dick really supposed to be in the dirt.

"Have them niggas to clean this nigga up and take him to go get Mini's money," Zion told Big Body before exiting the stinky basement.

Big Body walked him back upstairs. "You know too many niggas don't make it out of the dungeon, right? You just gave that lil' nigga a free pass."

"He made a mistake on some young nigga shit. You can tell he ain't about that life for real, so I gave him another chance to do better. Why kill a kid that got potential to do good in this world? I doubt he going back down the wrong path after this... Everything ain't punishable by death, nigga," Zion stated before climbing into the back of the truck.

"That's some real shit, and I respect that, but I'm not the one that made shit like this out here. That's the structure J-Rock put in place," Big Body agreed before dapping him up.

"Watch how you move out here, bruh. We about to start doing more good around this muthafucka."

Big Body nodded. "Alright now. Take your ass on to that gym. I got these streets, fool."

Zion closed the truck door and let the window down. "Got to give back to the streets sometimes and stop taking away so much. Fuck what J-Rock put in place. He ain't here. This your community. You need to step up and really get involved like a mayor," he preached before rolling his window back up.

He looked at Big Body as the driver slowly backed out

of the uneven concrete driveway. Big Body needed some-body to tell him what it was and keep it real with him. He had way too many people around that feared him too much to tell him what was on their minds. Every leader needed a nigga like Zion to keep them humble.

CHAPTER 35

MURK

MURK DID A SURPRISE POP-UP AT A TRAINING FACILITY downtown. It was built like a stylish football dome but was really ran like a military base by two badass Irish brothers. The facility was generally contracted by various sections of the military to train and weaponize delinquent soldiers. It was basically like a boot camp for soldiers that still had potential to be a viable asset to the military. That was ironic because the brothers were both delinquents back during their times in the service.

It was definitely a restricted establishment, but they made an exception for Murk and the Vultures. They were the *only* people outside of the military that had unsupervised clearance to enter the facility.

Murk went through security in the lobby and made his way inside. There were a dozen training sections in the huge building, and all of them were advanced. There was a section that imitated a beach during a sea storm with the heavy wave current in the water, then there was another section that imitated a tropical jungle with all the key elements. Those were two of the most popular sections, but Murk's favorite was the busy city section. It was perfect for him and fit his line of work.

"Ahhhh! You trying to slip past me, huh?" Ronnie asked from behind.

Murk spun around and laid eyes on his muscular Irish friend. He was one of the few people he actually considered a friend these days. "Nahhh, bruh! You know it ain't never like that. I know yo' ass be busy running this wild mutha-fucka. I'm here by myself today, just about to get me a lil' therapy session in."

"Nonsense, bro! Always good to see a good friend but go ahead and get your session. I got some fresh meat on the way, about to break them in!" Ronnie shouted before walking away in his tactical gear, assault rifle in hand.

Murk smiled as he thought about the night they crossed paths.

Ronnie was the wildcard out of the two brothers. His brother, David, was more of a lowkey type, so they didn't hang around each other all the time. That particular night, Ronnie was on the eastside, partying at this club by himself. It was one of those diverse clubs that attracted different crowds.

Murk was there with Swiss and two other Vultures, enjoying the night. They were chilling in their own little VIP section, in their own little world. It was Ronnie's ass who was on the dance floor drunk as hell, dancing wildly. He ended up bumping into this Hispanic dude, and shit got really wild from there. All Hispanics ran deep in Charlotte, and Ronnie was about to find out for himself.

Murk peeped the whole play and just watched it untold. To his surprise, Ronnie dealt the first blow as the Hispanic ranted about disrespect. All hell broke loose from there. Even dead drunk, Ronnie knocked out all five Hispanics right there in the middle of the club. The DJ cut the music, and the rest of the crowd backed up and had their phones out, recording the whole thing.

Ronnie's party vibe was obviously ruined, so he picked up his now cracked phone off of the floor and left. Murk quickly got up and caught up to him in the parking lot.

"Yooo! Say, bruh!" Murk called out to the big, white man.

Ronnie spun around quickly and came up with his pistol in the same motion. "Not another step!"

"Woahhh!" Murk said while putting both hands in the air. "I'm not against you, bruh."

"Drop your guns or I'll shoot him dead in the eye! I never miss!" Ronnie shouted sternly at Murk's Vultures, who made their way up the parking lot with their guns trained on Ronnie.

Murk looked back. "Nahhh! We ain't on that tonight, bruh! Y'all put the guns up now!" Murk shouted just as sternly, and they quickly tucked their guns.

"What do you want?" Ronnie asked Murk curiously, noticeably impressed with his authority over his men.

"I seen you handle yourself in there, and seeing how you handle that pistol tells me everything I need to know... I'm not even going to hold you up. Me and my fellas need that type of training. We're the clean-up crew out here, and

we keep order within the city. Military training will put us on the level that I need us to be on, so we can accomplish the shit we accomplish much easier. Just ask around the city about Rock Nation if you don't believe me. My name is Murk, and I'm the top Vulture."

Ronnie nodded slowly. "I'm going to do just that, and I'll be back in touch with you if you check out," he promised before tucking his pistol and hopping into his black Chevy pickup.

Ronnie had done his homework and reached out to Murk about a week after that. He was impressed with Murk and the fear his name brought in the streets. He was a ruthless warrior, and of course Ronnie saw the potential in him and his crew. That was about two years ago, and Murk couldn't thank himself enough for chasing Ronnie down that night. Just as he'd predicated, Ronnie's training made a world of difference. It made the Vultures street gods and undoubtedly extended their run in the streets.

Murk headed into the City Warfare Zone and headed straight to the locker room after grabbing some protective gear from the manager in front. Although they only used silicone bullets in training, you still didn't want those bullets piercing your skin. He suited up and prepared to get him a good session in. He had to release some stress.

T he training session lasted for forty minutes. Murk made an impressive score on the course and got a good workout in, but he still hadn't relieved himself.

Back in the locker room, he took off his equipment and hopped in the shower. After the steaming shower, he threw on another jogging suit and exited the facility. He didn't run into Ronnie on his way out, but he left a message for him with the receptionist.

"Let me head over to my side of town," he said to himself before hopping in his shiny, black, 2016 Jeep Grand Cherokee SRT. He zipped swiftly through traffic and was on the eastside of Charlotte before he knew it.

Swiss was a captain and a made man in his own right, but he refused to leave the hood. Whenever they weren't on a mission, he bounced between different apartment complexes within their hood. He was a brick baby, and he was content with being hood-rich because he didn't plan on ever leaving the hood.

Swiss was throwing a big ass cookout at their new headquarters. Eastway Crossing Apartments was notorious for its front street location. It was right off of Eastway Drive, one of the busiest streets on that side of town. Eastway Crossing was a new development around the way, and Swiss saw the potential early on.

He shared his vision with Murk, and Murk got behind him. They locked in with the complex manager and secured ten permanent apartment units before the grand opening a few years ago. Murk, Swiss, and two of their lieutenants had apartments. The other six were rented to Rock Nation as stash houses. Tory kept most of the money there. It was the most secure place and the closest they'd ever come to getting out of the hood.

Swiss kept the apartments running smoothly. He kept

all the tenants happy and was the reason the young eastside jack boys didn't kick down doors in Eastway Crossing.

"Yooo!" Swiss shouted after rounding the corner to the middle of the complex where the pool and picnic area was.

The eastside of Charlotte was hood but diverse at the same time. There was plenty of Black people that stayed out there, but there was also a few white and Hispanic families. They all lived in peace and harmony without the threat of raising their kids in crime. Eastway Drive had become the safest neighborhood on the eastside, and that was all thanks to the Vultures.

Everybody showed love to Murk, greeting him verbally and physically. Besides Swiss and two soldiers he had with him, everyone else outside was a civilian — regular people who clocked in and worked hard every day. They were blind to most things about Vulture business, but they knew they were up under their protection and that they should be grateful to them.

"You out here vibing hard today, I see," Murk noted as he approached Swiss.

Swiss was over by the pool, grilling chicken, without a care in the world. It was still too chilly to swim, so it wasn't a pool party. It was just a cookout, and the best grill in the complex just so happened to be around the pool.

"Why not? It's a beautiful day. You don't see all this sun shining on this watch, nigga?" Swiss boasted before holding up the iced out, platinum, Cartier watch on his left wrist.

Murk nodded his approval. His homie was definitely cleaner than a box of Gain with his black, designer jeans outfit. "Yeah, the weather is bipolar as hell this year, but I see you, fool... Got the hoes out here today, I see."

"Hell yeah, nigga! Spring break on the way crazy, man. You know them college girls love to party," Swiss said before flipping some chicken over. You could tell he was just getting the hang of the grilling thing.

"I see. I just might stick around for this one."

Swiss gave him a weird look. "Whattt? I know Almighty Murk ain't about to shoot the shit. Not Mr. Workaholic himself."

"I got to hop on a plane for my Uncle Timbo baby shower in the morning. Might as well chill for tonight. It's some bad bitches out here," he said while eye fucking a few of them at a table nearby.

He had on a black, Nike, jogging suit with no jewelry. That was his swag, and he liked it that way. Most people on the outside looking in thought that Swiss was the boss of the two because he was flashier. That was just the way of the world, and Murk understood that. If it wasn't for the expensive cars he drove, you would think he was a regular person.

"You ain't told me Timbo had an ole lady."

Murk nodded his head. "Shit, they moved fast! He told me something about the bitch, and next thing you know, I'm getting death threats from Timbo."

"I can hear that nigga now, cussing yo' ass out. Wassup? I'm trying to slide out that way too, nigga. Miami got some good ass weather right now."

Murk shook his head. "Nahhh! I need you out here pimpin'. You got to hold it down while I'm gone. I'll be gone for a few days."

"Aight, I got you... I see you eye fucking them bitches over there. Swear, I been over here plotting on they ass too," Swiss admitted while locking in on them himself.

Murk reached his hand out for a shake. "They keep peeping over here, so I know they see us watching... Yeah, we about to fuck all them tonight. Two for me, two for you."

CHAPTER 36

ICE

LIEUTENANT JACKSON AND HIS MEN DECIDED TO PLEDGE their allegiance to Ice and his empire. Ice kept his word and gave them the condo that he first met them at. Ice didn't waste any time. He instantly drew up a play and thought up the best way to get back at Big Body. Niggas only respected retaliation in their world, so Ice had to get with the program.

"Let me get this right. You're both a part of the same organization, but you're arch enemies?" LT asked.

Ice nodded his head. He could tell LT just wanted to know every detail, so he could assess the entire situation. "Exactly. Like it be whole wars going on within the organization. The shit so wicked out here; it's like a game. Really hard to explain to be honest."

"Sounds like you need to switch locations," LT suggested with shrugged shoulders.

"Nahhh." Ice shook his head. "I thought about it a few times but can't bring myself to do it. I was born and raised out here in Charlotte. This is my base of operations and my fort. I can't leave the fort, bruh. I got to hold this mutha-fucka down. You should be able to understand that."

LT nodded his head, obviously satisfied with Ice's response. "A stand-up type of man is a man that I can trust and respect."

They sat in the food court of Ice Cold Fun House, enjoying a meal like two normal people. Ice couldn't show him the secret headquarters, so they met there. Both dressed casually and neither wore jewelry.

"Yeah. I might not be America's next top gangsta, but I'm definitely a solid nigga who gone definitely get me some money and take care of his," Ice informed matter-of-factly.

LT nodded his approval.

"I'm glad we're on the same page. Now, we can get down to the business." Ice paused for effect. "I just want to be perfectly clear right now before we really lock in and seal the deal."

"Talk to me," LT encouraged gently but looked at him through a hard stare.

"You're going to be responsible for the safety of my empire, and that means eliminating all possible and definite threats. Big Body has to go immediately."

LT leaned in a little closer to him over the table before he spoke. "When you say he has to go, you're talking about putting him down, right?"

"Fucking right! This shit is serious out here, bruh. If you see a threat, you got to kill it before you end up dead," Ice said before sipping his raspberry slushy. "I don't want to do it, but that nigga got to go. Y'all get thirty-thousand-dollar bonuses if y'all get the job done within the week."

"He's a killer, right? Like a ruthless individual?" LT asked for more reassurance.

Ice locked eyes with him and nodded his head definitively. "Hell yeah! You ain't just got to take my word for it either. Ask who you want to ask. Big Body been a plague on the westside for years. You won't be losing no blessings by taking his shiesty ass off the map."

"You ain't got to say another word, boss man," LT assured while rubbing his beard. "Might as well go ahead and get those payments ready. We want everything wire transferred. We don't deal in cash," he informed before getting up and walking off toward the exit.

Ice leaned back in his seat and watched LT as he walked off. A slow smile started from the inside of his soul and ended up on his face. He was excited and anxious to see how LT and his men were going to get the job done.

CHAPTER 37
LANEY

LANEY STRAIGHTENED UP AROUND THE HOUSE A LITTLE AND worked the hell out of the movers who delivered the rest of their furniture. It was going to take a lot more placements and decorations to make the house complete, but it was definitely coming along nicely.

She couldn't believe they had a house in walking distance from Ta'Jae. It was unbelievable still. The feeling of accomplishment felt so good to her, and it showed on the outside. She was literally glowing.

The baby oil she had just applied to her sexy, brown skin made her glow even more than she already was naturally. She had on a sexy, little, skimpy nurse's costume as she laid on the big bed, scrolling through her iPhone comfortably. Her hair was freshly done from the day before, and she had on a new pair of stiletto heels that she'd been looking for an excuse to wear. Well, tonight was the night.

Zion walked into their bedroom and dropped his gym

bad on the floor before stopping to stare at her. "Damn, girl! You ain't tell me you had all this goodness waiting here for a nigga."

She didn't turn around to look at him or nothing. She didn't budge, but he couldn't see the sneaky smile on her face because her back was to him.

"Oh, you want to play games with a real nigga tonight, huh?" he said with satisfaction.

She bit her bottom lip as she heard him getting closer. "Ahhhh!" she screamed once he grabbed one of her ankles and quickly pulled her to the edge of the bed where he stood.

Laney turned around to look up at her man and literally melted. It wasn't as intense as their first night being body to body, but he made her melt every time. The way he handled her body in his hands and stared at her during intimate connections made her short of breath.

He was doing it right then — rubbing his hands up and down her moist thighs while staring daggers down at her. She tossed her phone across the bed and tried her best to maintain eye contact with him. It was difficult for her to do in times like that, but she always rose to the challenge.

"You gone stand there and babysit the pussy, or you going to beat this pussy?" she asked devilishly, challenging him directly.

He smiled back at her with his own evil little smirk before yanking her a little closer to him. She was halfway off of the bed, but he held her up. "Looks like I'm going to have one more fight I got to win before the day is over with."

"Uhmmmmmmm! You going to knock this pussy out, baby?" she asked with seductive humor.

"You know what I do," he responded before pushing her back onto the bed and pushing her legs up over her head.

He folded her up into a lazy pretzel and started to lick and suck the skin off of her clit. He fingered her pussy at the same time, and before she knew it, she was pissing squirt all over his face.

He picked her up off of the bed when she was done and held her eye to eye with him. "I still can't believe we right here in each other's arms. You motivated me to do what I had to do to get out of that muthafucka early, and I can't thank you enough for giving a nigga so much to look forward to."

"Awwww! Nigga, you *know* I love when you get all sentimental, especially while we being intimate," she said before leaning in to kiss him passionately on his big, pretty, pink lips.

He kissed her back as he continued to hold her in the air in his arms. He took his free hand and pulled her thong to the side, so he could drop her down onto his curved dick.

"Oooowwwweeee! I love how that damn dick feel in me," she admitted as she clasped her hands around his neck. She was prepared for the ride.

Zion used the perfect motion when navigating her guts as always. It amazed her how he automatically knew his way around her body from the inside out without her having to even give him a hint.

She bit her lip and gladly took the dick he was dishing out. His dick wasn't as big as her previous sneaky link, but it was big enough, and she didn't have not one complaint. For her, the dick was better when she actually loved the nigga that it was connected to.

"Bounce me on that dick, baby! I want to feel it in my chest, nigga!" she challenged with a little aggression.

"Aight, bitch! I got you!" he complied before getting in demon mode his damn self.

They were both in that mode that night and literally fucked each other's brains out. Zion was already worn out from a big day at the gym, so of course she put his ass to sleep. He lasted a good forty minutes though, and he put *a lot* of work in before he checked out, so she couldn't complain.

She just laid there, naked, in his arms, listening to him snore up a storm. "Lord, please look over this damn man. Don't know what I'd do if I lost his ass. You brought him home to me safely. *Please* keep him here."

After sending her prayer up to the sky, she got up out of the bed, so she could get a quick shower in. She wanted to hurry up and get back in the bed with her man. It was one of those nights where you knew you were about to get some of the best sleep of your life. She was about to cherish it too.

CHAPTER 38

TORY

IT MIGHT'VE BEEN AN ORDINARY MONDAY NIGHT FOR THE average Charlotte citizen, but for Tory, every day was unordinary. He dealt hundreds of thousands of dollars a day, so his days were different. He was currently in the process of showing Careesha the ropes. The thought of having her around actually grew on him overnight because he saw her maximum potential.

With her close under his wing, he could mold her into a real boss bitch that would become an invaluable asset to him in the long run. She was a boss bitch in her own right, but it was levels to the game. Tory was about to put her on a higher shelf, but first, he had to make sure she was truly worthy, so he planned to keep her as close as possible in the meantime. It wouldn't take too long for him to figure out if she was trustworthy.

"What the hell is this, Tory?" Careesha asked with a crumbled face while looking down at the paper folder he placed in her lap once she got in the passenger's seat of his

Lamborghini truck. He had just picked her up from her house. She would be his passenger princess for the day.

"That's work, muthafucka!" he answered with extra matter-of-factness. "Hard muthafuckin' work... That's a list of all the delivery drop-off spots throughout North Carolina and the surrounding states. Up until now, we ain't been really offering delivery services. Thanks to you and your crew, I was forced to create new jobs. Fortunately for y'all, those jobs was needed."

She looked down at the folder and back at his ass with a roll of her large eyeballs. "If you ain't want me to be out here, you should've just said that. I came out here to stay out here, not to get sent on the fuckin' road."

"Hahaha!" He laughed aloud while looking over at her little fine ass. She only had on jeans and a sweater, but her clothes hugged her body and showed her full slim-thick figure. Her curly, long wig, along with the perfume she wore, had Tory very satisfied with her presence. "Let me find out you came out here to be up under a nigga."

Those pretty eyes were rolled once more. "Yeah, I did, but don't get the big head, nigga... I want to be around you, so I can learn the game on a higher level than what I'm used to. I'm trying to elevate, Tory."

"I know, nigga," he assured. "The thing is... that delivery business is going to be your first step toward elevation. That's a lot of fuckin responsibility too, so you should be happy right now. Plus, I'm putting you in charge of the business. You're responsible for making sure each package gets where it needs to be and the cash gets back here. You're a manager, so you don't have to hit the road yourself. Just make sure your people are reliable, and you won't have shit to worry about," he assured before cranking the Lamborghini up and backing out of her driveway slowly.

Careesha nodded her head in satisfaction with her glossy bottom lip poking out. "I can get jiggy with that right there, nigga. You must've known I wasn't going for no bullshit because you damn sure set a bitch up *realllll nice*," she finished with a full smile, plenty of teeth and tongue showing.

"Shut the hell up before I slap yo' lil' ass on the cleaning detail," he threatened before turning on the music.

Dej Loaf's new hit single, *No Fear,* began to bump through the speakers, and Tory turned it up to full blast. He began to bop his head and do a little upper body two step while driving that only got more hype as the tempo built up on the song.

"Wooooow! Not the big, bad Tory vibing to some shit like this," she chastised with a bright smile on her face. She was obviously impressed by his versatility.

He looked over at her with a smile of his own. "Shut the hell up!"

CHAPTER 39
GLOCK

Today was the day that Glock had been waiting on all damn week. He'd been training at the gun range with his gang and planning for their future. Friday came around slower than usual, but it was probably only because he was anticipating it so much.

He grew a heart earlier in the week and vacated Dang's premises. Dang had been severely cooperative since his arrival. Plus, he didn't like houses like that. He was an apartment baby and literally felt better when living in an apartment complex. He never felt right when sleeping in a house. That was why he never visited his grandmother how he should've when she moved out of the apartments.

Forestcrest Apartments were the biggest set of apartments in town, and Glock liked how it was set up. It wasn't hidden like Glock City back in Charlotte, but it was definitely a nice little set up. It wasn't front street, and the police rarely came out there unless they were called.

Forestcrest was filled to capacity after he sent his niggas to get the last few vacant units, so he had to do what he had to do. He overpaid a family to move out of one of the three-bedroom units. There weren't too many of those, so you know Glock had to get a VIP unit. The family was happy to take the money and was moved out the very next day.

The Glockians were still adapting to the slow motion out there in Durham, but no one complained because they were out there in the name of Glock. It was a warm, sunny day, and all fourteen of them lounged in the front of Glock's new apartment building, waiting for orders. Music was playing, the grill was going, kids were running around, and all. Glock knew all eyes were on the new hoodlums in town, so he had to win the people over.

That was the easy part though. The rent was only three hundred and fifty dollars a month out there, and there were fifty units. He wasn't rich, but he could afford the seventeen thousand it took to complete the task. The community showed their gratitude every time he came outside, and his plan was working like a charm so far — the first phase of his plan anyway. The second phase's success would be determined on that day.

Glock emerged from his apartment dressed in a black Ralph Lauren t-shirt and skinny, black jeans. He had on black Air Force 1s that matched his black bookbag, which held his AK-47. His Glock was tucked in the waistband of his pants. You would think he was on the way to get busy on some gangster shit, but he was only heading to a meeting. That was just how Glock moved, and his gang eagerly followed suit.

"You ready?" Ruga asked after walking up to Glock with similar attire on.

Glock nodded his head. "I been waiting on this day for a whole week... That's them?" he asked while nodding toward the white Kia car on the other side of the parking lot.

Ruga nodded. "Yeah. They just pulled up a few minutes ago. I told 'em to wait for you right there."

"Let's do it. Might as well ride with them," Glock decided suddenly before leading the way across the parking lot toward Kelsey's car.

She stepped out of the car as they approached and adjusted her clothing. She had on a Victoria's Secret sweatsuit that was a little on the loose side, but nothing she wore could hide her curvy figure. Her puffy fro was curlier than ever, and Glock had to shake himself out of her trance as they approached because he always found himself getting lost in her natural beauty. "I see you in dress code today."

Kelsey shot him a smile. "Boy, I did not wear black because of you and your little gang colors. I woke up and decided to wear black all on my own," she informed matter-of-factly.

"Yeahhhhh, aighttt!" he replied with clear skepticism.

She shook her head at him. Her smile remained on her face. "So, are you going to follow us to the meeting spot, or do you want to ride with me?"

Glock answered her question by walking past her and hopping in the backseat of her car. Ruga walked around to the passenger's side and did the same. Kelsey hopped back in the driver's seat and put on her seatbelt.

"Word around town is y'all came out here and took over these apartments," she informed casually.

Glock shrugged. "We just turned it up a little bit. If the owner was smart, he'd get some more apartments built in that empty field down the road."

"That's actually a good idea because this complex is overly crowded," Kelsey's Caucasian passenger chimed in.

Glock looked at her and smiled. "Wassup, Snow Bunny? You must be Alexis? Kelsey told me a lil' something about you... I'm not even going to lie. You look better than I pictured in my head," he said teasingly.

"Thank you. I guess," Alexis responded awkwardly.

"Girl, he literally says anything out of his mouth, and I told you he loves to chastise people," Kelsey assured her friend to lighten the mood.

She quickly turned on the music and pulled out of the parking spot before Glock could chastise her further.

———

About thirty minutes later, they were pulling into a small local diner on the other side of town. The Blacks called it Cracker Town, and the whites called the Black side of town Monkey Town. Glock had never been to such a racist place before, but he was slowly beginning to understand the way of things around there. It wasn't new. It had been going on for generations.

"This your first time around these parts?" Alexis asked them curiously.

Glock nodded. "Yeah... I'm ready to leave already. Too many white people make me nervous."

"I swear!" Ruga agreed strongly. "Nigga ain't even trying to go inside that muthafucka. It's thirty white folks in there. We going to stick out like hard nipples."

Kelsey laughed. "Don't worry. You're guests of the sheriff, and he runs this town. No one will bother you or even look at you twice. You're here for a meeting. That's all."

"Yeah, but you're going to have to leave your guns in the car though. Can't go inside the diner with them," Alexis strongly advised while turning around and looking at them.

Ruga looked over at Glock, who was contemplating. He'd never went any place but jail without at least a pistol. He knew the sheriff wouldn't harm them though, so he made up his mind. "Man, let's get this shit over with," he spat before pulling the Glock out of his waistband.

They all got out of the car and made their way into the diner. As expected, every eyeball in the place was trained on them. Not only one but three Black people walked in with Alexis, and that just wasn't usual.

Despite all the attention, Glock and Ruga didn't seem fazed in the least. They just followed Alexis and Kelsey to the wraparound booth in the corner of the diner where the sheriff sat in full uniform. He was one of those tall, muscular rednecks that was built solid since a kid and toted concrete blocks in the air and flipped big tires for fun.

"You two, have a seat," the sheriff said to Glock and Ruga. "You two, wait for us over there," he instructed Kelsey and Alexis while motioning toward the stools by the dining counter.

Ruga slid into the sitting booth first, then Glock sat on

the outer side. "You must be Sheriff Dowell," said Glock once he was comfortably seated.

The sheriff nodded. "That's me, and you must be Glock. The good pastor has told me some interesting things about you and the people you run with. I can't even deny that... That's why you're here right now. If even half of the shit he says about you is true, then that would make you a credible threat, and I'm not a man to take threats lightly, son. State your business in my town."

Glock released a deep breath. "I'm not your son! Let's get that clear off top... And as far as my business, it's pretty clear. I'm here to free the fucking slaves in this town. At first, it was business for me, but now, it's personal."

"Oh, yeah?" Dowell asked through laughter. He started laughing even harder when he was done speaking. He obviously heard a joke somewhere in Glock's last statement.

"Yeah, nigga. I ain't stutter! I'm just here to tell you to stay out of my way. Let me humble those Aryans without your interference. Let's see how big and bad they are without your protection."

The sheriff shook his head while looking at Glock with an amused expression. "We've had this system set up out here for decades. You think you're going to just pop up out here and regulate something? You're sadly mistaken, son."

Glock started to respond, but Dowell raised his index finger. "Listen, y'all might be used to throwing your weight around everywhere else, but this town is a stronghold. My best advice to you is to try it somewhere else. It's not going to end well for you... That's a polite warning and some sound advice for you right there."

"With all due respect, Sheriff, fuck your advice," Glock

retorted seriously while staring the sheriff dead in his light blue eyes. "I'm not asking you for advice, and I don't listen to warnings. I'm just trying to see if you and your deputies going to take this thirty thousand dollars to fall back while I put the press on your lil' guard dogs. I heard they was big and bad, and I'm here to put that to the test."

"That's your death sentence," Dowell predicated matter-of-factly.

Glock slid out of the booth and stood up to his feet. "I know if you don't stay out of my way, it just might be yo' muthafuckin' funeral!" he threatened seriously, and he meant *every* word. He was all in, and there was no turning back at this point.

The sheriff stood, towering over Glock, and Ruga got to his feet as well. A few local men stood up as well, and the diner had turned dead silent. The tension in the air was thicker than a Black Friday crowd, and Kelsey obviously wasn't having that.

"Everybody just chill out!" she spat after wedging herself between Glock and the sheriff. "Damn! Y'all acting like some little kids. Can't even carry on a decent conversation without bumping heads... You're here to offer him a deal," she said to Glock.

"This nigga don't want the money! What the fuck I'm supposed to do? I'm still gone handle my business. He just better stay the fuck out of my way!" Glock spat heatedly. He refused to fold — or bend — for the white man.

"You're going to die out here, son," Dowell promised through clenched teeth.

"Alright. How about this... He's so bad and tough, right?" she said to Dowell. "If he can take care of the

Swamp Bullies, then you let him do his thing with the Aryans unbothered."

Sheriff Dowell's eyes lit up at the idea, and that didn't go unnoticed by Glock. "Young lady, that's a brilliant idea... If y'all can do something about those damn swamp people, you can have your way with the Aryans."

Glock's squinted eyes moved back-and-forth between Kelsey and the sheriff, who were both waiting on his response. He didn't know anything about the swamp people, but he didn't fear a soul, so of course he accepted. He just wanted to complete his mission. "Fuck them folks! I'll show you how me and mines get down!"

The sheriff nodded his head slowly. "Good luck, lil' fellow."

"Call them and wish them luck. They the ones that's gone need it," Glock spat confidently before exiting the diner with Ruga close behind.

CHAPTER 40

BIG BODY

Knock! Knock! Knock!

Big Body was torn out of a deep slumber by someone knocking on his car window. He had fallen asleep in the parking lot of a local gas station. "Wassup, wassup?" he spat as he gained consciousness.

"You out here lacking, big bruh," one of his young street soldiers warned seriously. His window was cracked a little. "I knew it was your ass too. You the only nigga on the westside with a lime green Porsche."

He was parked on the side of a Shell gas station around the way. It was a nice day outside, so he decided to flex the Porsche since it was warming up.

"Mannnn, that new batch of lean is strong as fuck, lil' bruh," he informed truthfully in a slow, groggy tone. "Want some of this shit?"

The youngin shook his head rapidly. "Hell nah, big bruh! I can't afford to sleep like you, nigga. I got to be up out here on the block. Just had another baby boy."

"Damn, lil' nigga!" Big Body spat after taking another sip from his doubled Styrofoam cup. "You seventeen with three kids already? Yeah, slow your lil' ass down, lil' nigga. Been done lost all your hair by the time you turn twenty-five at this rate. Them kids ain't no joke, lil' bruh."

Big Body was the biggest it got on the westside, and most young niggas were scared to even approach him directly. It wasn't ideal, but the young nigga had always been special since a kid. He was fearless and wise beyond his years. Big Body had a soft spot for the lil' nigga. His name was Shiesty, and he was very popular in the neighborhood. Everybody loved the lil' nigga. He had a genuineness about himself like the rapper Lil Boosie, but he was handsome like Trey Songz.

"Them kids is my legacy, bruh. Promise I'm gone leave an empire behind for they ass," Shiesty retorted matter-of-factly.

Big Body smiled up at the young nigga, showcasing his flawless diamond grill. "Get in the car, youngin'. It's about that time you graduated in these streets. You seem like you ready to take on more responsibility out here and fly up under my wing. It's that time, fool."

Lil' Shiesty grinned evilly before making his way around to the passenger's seat. He favored the rapper, NBA Youngboy, when he smiled. They had the same grin for sure.

"This bitch smell like a new shoe box," Shiesty joked after closing the car door behind himself. "Can't wait until I'm living like this."

"Just stay down, bruh. I swear that footwork gone pay off. Especially with me on your ass now. You really ain't got shit to worry about, lil' nigga. All you got to do is stay out of jail and that damn graveyard," he promised before cranking up the engine and turning the music up louder.

He shook the grogginess off from the lean and pulled out of the parking space. He had some business to handle on the other side of town, and he decided to bring Shiesty along with him. He wasn't about to waste any time. It was Shiesty's time to step up.

It would've been easier for him to hop on the freeway to get to his destination, but he tried to avoid that route at all costs these days. The state troopers were on the bullshit this time of year, and he didn't have time for all of that, so he happily took the street way. It was mostly back roads. He knew the city like his own dick.

He had stopped at a stop sign, on a back street on the westside, so he could twist a joint real quick. He gave Shiesty his own weed to twist up, so neither of them saw the white car pull up alongside them. By the time Big Body looked up, it was way too late. He was staring down the barrels of two semi-automatic rifles.

"Fuckkk!" was the very last word that Big Body would ever speak in his life.

Gunshots erupted immediately after that, and the quiet neighborhood block was turned into a marching band parade. The military grade rifles were monstrous and easily tore through the Porsche like stabbing a sheet of paper with sharpened pencils. The two masked shooters emptied fifty rounds apiece without even hopping out of the car.

The car sped off after the deed was done, leaving a bunch of empty shells on the ground and big holes in the

Porsche. Both Big Body and Lil' Shiesty were slumped over, covered in their own blood.

CHAPTER 41

TORY

"THE STREETS AIN'T THE SAME NO MORE, SO LUCKILY FOR you, we about to cut down on clientele. Mainly the recent ones. Just going to have them shopping with the main clientele," said Tory while pacing the hardwood floor in his townhouse on the westside.

Careesha sat on top of the bar counter that was connected to the kitchen because he hadn't had the chance to furnish the place yet. "Okay. So, you're basically just limiting access, right?"

"Exactly! I don't trust all them folks, so I'm about to cut the grass. Anybody who don't make the cut is going to have to go through a middleman. Some of them going to have to go through two," he decided.

It was his job to build and protect Rock Nation's drug empire, and he took that job very seriously. He refused to appear incompetent, so he tried to stay a few steps ahead of every curve.

"I'm not going to lie. That's a smart move. Putting the

responsibility and work on your most trusted clients. They'll be more than happy for the responsibility because it comes with more money."

He stopped pacing and looked across the room at his latest crush. Careesha was learning fast, and she was good at analyzing the game from a higher position. It was like she had a gift for observing the field, and Tory planned on seeing just how good she could be. Over the next few months, he planned to keep her under his wing and push her to the limit.

"What, nigga?" she spat once she looked up and noticed him staring.

She had on tight sweatpants with a halter top to match, and the way she had her hair pinned up in a Japanese bun did something to him. She was a straight-up hood princess, but at the same time, she still had class about herself. It was nowhere near Laney's level of class, but she was still classy in a ghetto type of way. It was the perfect mixture for a gutter nigga like himself.

"I ain't even going to lie. Yo' lil' ass need to let me take you out to dinner tonight. Know this nice lil' Hibachi spot over on the southside we can hit up. They got mini golf and all," he suggested with a straight face, so she'd know he wasn't bullshitting.

She pursed her lips together and hit him with that adorable half-smile half-blush that women displayed when they were flattered and were left speechless. "Your phone's ringing, sir." It was vibrating on the counter right next to her.

"You can't run from this shit forever. You know you want a nigga too. Ain't gone find a nigga better for you," he assured as he made his way over to her. "This shit better be good, fool. Had Careesha right where the fuck I wanted her," he barked at Choppa upon answering the phone.

"He a muthafuckin' lie!" she spat playfully.

Tory waved her off with a smirk. "You heard what I said, nigga. Wassup though, bruh? Please tell me something good. I'm having a good day today."

"Mannnn, bruh!" Choppa said with a raspy and shaky voice. It was clear that he'd been crying, or was about to, and that raised Tory's adrenaline immediately.

He hadn't heard Choppa sound like that since his mother passed away years ago. "What the fuck happened, my nigga?! You good?"

"What happened?" Careesha asked urgently, picking up on his concern.

He stuck up his index finger at her, motioning for her to hold on. "Talk to me, bruh! Tell me what happened, my nigga! I can't fix it if you don't tell me what happened."

At that point, Choppa was sobbing uncontrollably, and it tore at Tory's heart because he loved the nigga like a brother. They shared the same pain, so he was automatically hurt even though he didn't even know what was wrong yet.

"Choppa, you got to talk to me, man!" he pushed with urgency.

"They took Big Body!" he blurted out abruptly, like it was hard to say. "He's gone, bruh!"

Tory's face crumbled like a motorcycle under a big truck as he pulled the phone away from his face to look at it. "What the fuck you mean? The police snatched him up or something?"

"He's gone-gone, bruh! They shot him up in his car. He dead, Tory! He gone, bruhhh!" Choppa informed regretfully before bursting back into a fit of sobs.

Tory dropped his phone on the floor and took a deep breath. He stood there, openmouthed, with tears racing down his face. He was temporarily paralyzed.

Careesha quickly hopped off of the counter and embraced him. That little comfort was all it took. He tried to fight it, but the pain was too heavy for his heart. He broke all the way down in her arms. His heart was broken into a thousand pieces.

CHAPTER 42

LANEY

LANEY WAS WOKEN UP OUT OF HER NAP BY LESTER. HE had moved into the mansion with her, so he could be in-house security. Zion hired a few dudes from a private security firm for himself and a few more for Laney as well to help Lester out, but they were only on the clock when they were outside. Lester's job was 24/7.

"Laney, get up! Tory just called. Big Body got gunned down earlier. He's screaming for blood," he informed while shaking her out of a deep slumber.

Laney was getting some of the best sleep of her life. Zion had put that dick down on her before he left for the gym earlier, but when she heard those words come out of Lester's mouth, she popped up like a dick in a strip club. She was praying it was a dream, but unfortunately, it wasn't. She shook her head rapidly then looked up at Lester with wide eyes. "Pleaseeee tell me this is a bad prank, bruh. Please tell me that ain't true."

Lester pursed his lips together and shook his head slowly.

"Fuckkkkkk, mannn!" she barked abruptly with surprising force before popping up out of the bed.

She shot past a startled Lester into her closet, so she could throw something quick on. She had to hurry up and hit the streets, so she could control the storm. BBG was not a force to be reckoned with whatsoever. Big Body kept them in line and maintained structure amongst the savages. As wicked as he was, he was severely needed in her operation. He served a bigger purpose in the community than most people recognized.

"Hello!" she spat once Murk answered his phone. It sounded like he'd been taking an afternoon nap himself.

"What you want, girl?" he asked as he let out a long stretch.

"Listen here, nigga! Get yo' muthafuckin' ass up *right now*! This a state of emergency right here. Big Body just got gunned down on the westside, and we need to get ahead of this tornado and prevent it. I'm not about to have a civil war on my watch, so you need to get all your Vultures and meet me on the westside. I got to hit the field and get hands on!" she spat while pulling some black jeans onto her ass.

"Damn, that ain't pretty for nobody. Got to find somebody to take his spot quick," Murk advised. He didn't sound tired anymore either. The news had torn him awake as well.

"Exactly! Hurry up, round up them troops, and meet me at the Walmart on his side. We'll ride into their hood as one," she instructed before hanging up the call and throwing on a black hoodie.

———

Alittle later that evening, Murk showed up to the Walmart parking lot appropriately — eight cars deep, full of soldiers. Laney had Lester with her and three of her own security guards. She got word that Tory was already in the hood holding court, and she couldn't have that. Tory was unstable at the moment and moving off his emotions.

They headed out of the Walmart parking lot and rolled to Sandhurst as one. When they finally pulled into the complex, she saw that she had made the right decision to pull up with an army of her own because Tory definitely had the whole BBG out there. You would think there was a million-dollar prize giveaway by the amount of people in the apartment complex.

"This ain't good," said Lester from the driver's seat as he maneuvered through the many cars double-parked in the parking lot. "I can feel the tension in the air from the car."

"Hold on, slow down," she told him before rolling down the back window. "Where the fuck is Tory?" she asked a group of young wolves. "And stop looking at me all crazy. I'm running Rock Nation right now, and I don't got time for games. If y'all don't tell me where Tory at right now, I'm gone have them Vultures behind me see to y'all personally!" She had murder in her eyes and malice in her tone.

"He in the back by the basketball courts," one of them blurted out immediately, obviously not willing to call her bluff.

She sat back in her seat and rolled the window back up

without so much as a thank you. Lester led the motorcade through the complex and parked at the end of the driveway. You had to walk the rest of the way to get to the basketball courts.

Laney and the Vultures hopped out and left their vehicles lined up in the middle of the parking lot. All eyes were on them, and Laney didn't mind. She wanted to make a show of force and make her presence known. She pulled her hoodie over her head and walked over to Murk with sparkling black Ugg boots on her feet. She was the prettiest gangsta, and muthafuckas were going to learn that day.

"Y'all ready?" she asked him while scanning the Vultures gearing up for whatever, causing more tension in the air. They were hopping out with big army guns that were only seen in the movies.

"Don't we look ready?" Murk boasted seriously and confidently while holding up his favorite AK-47.

Laney nodded and led the way to the basketball court. Men, women, boys, and girls made a way for the hostile group of individuals that approached. Laney walked confidently, with a purpose, and her head held high. She noticed Choppa tap Tory on his shoulder, letting him know that they were incoming.

By the looks of it, he was holding a meeting with the lieutenants and sergeants on the basketball court; everybody else lurked in the distance. That was until Tory made his way forward to confront them. Then they started closing in around them.

"Y'all might as well gone back where y'all came from!" Tory strongly advised. It wasn't a threat but definitely close to it. "This is BBG business."

Laney looked around, peeping the scene, then back at Tory. "Nah, you too emotional right now, plus I can't have you doing nothing stupid. We need to figure out who's going to step up for BBG, and it can't be you for obvious reasons. Now, if you want to help me do that, then you can assist, but otherwise, I'm sure there's some business you need to be handling for our Rock Nation business."

"What?!" Tory's face was scrambled up like someone dropped him in a sewer. "Bitch, you worried about the wrong thing! My big brother just got gunned down in his own fucking hood, and you right here worried about who's going to take his spot? Get the fuck out of my hood before I have y'all put out! This my shit! I'm gone run BBG! Fuck Rock Nation, fuck you, and fuck them niggas behind you!" he barked, getting angrier at every word.

Laney wanted to grab Murk's gun and shoot him right in the mouth, but that wouldn't end well at all, so she kept her composure. "Tory, I'm gone let that slide because you obviously hurting right now, but don't be stupid, nigga. You don't want to play that card right there."

"I done made up my mind! That last shipment I got is took too! It's smoke, and I'm gone apply pressure until I get the truth. It was either Ice, Glock, or Murk. I don't trust y'all. I can't trust y'all, so it's fuck y'all! Since I don't know who did it, I'm gunning at all three of y'all niggas!" He was looking past her at Murk now.

"I'm gone kill you before J-Rock can make it back to do it himself," Murk promised calmly and coldly.

"You think you bringing up J-Rock supposed to scare me or something? I'm gone call him after this and tell him what's up. If he ain't on what I'm on, then it's fuck his ass too! Either you with me or against me at this point! He can't dodge no bullets, and neither can y'all, so I advise y'all to get the fuck on before I cross one name off my list right now!" he said to Murk. He was deadly serious too. Laney saw it in his eyes.

"Bitch ass nigga, we can all die right now! I bet you we take half of y'all out before y'all take us out!" Murk challenged. She could tell he was dead serious too.

"Y'all shut the fuck up!" Laney spat with as much force as she could muster. She was just remembering about the tiny baby in her stomach. She couldn't go out like that. Zion would scorch the earth. "Nobody else is dying today. You just made your bed, Tory. You got to stand on that shit now. Hope your soldiers built for what's coming," she advised before leading the way back to the motorcade.

Murk caught up to her after exchanging a few last threats with Tory. "Yeah, that nigga done lost it. I got to take him out immediately. As much as I hate to admit it, he got the manpower to go up against Rock Nation."

"Just prepare for the worst and pull all the troops in from other cities. Any certified shooter needs to be on their way to Charlotte tonight. Tell Glock to bring his ass back out here too! We need all the help we can get. BBG is way bigger than I thought," she instructed then stated before opening the door to her Maserati.

Murk nodded his understanding. "You need to go ahead and make that call to J-Rock and get ahead of this before he does."

"Fuck J-Rock! He's not going to side with Tory because he's going against him. Let him call J-Rock. I don't care.

I'm busy trying to stop my city from turning into Afghanistan."

Murk nodded again. "You're right. He's a dead man walking. He let his emotions get the best of him, but I promise you I'm going to kill him before J-Rock gets a chance."

"Prepare to do that because I refuse to let him bring heat down on us," she commanded before climbing into her truck.

CHAPTER 43

MURK

MURK PARTED WAYS WITH LANEY, AND HE SENT MOST OF his Vultures away to tend to their own business until further notice. Swiss rode with him to go make a little stop though. He was in the passenger's seat of Swiss' black Range Rover, and he decided to go ahead and call Glock while he had some free time.

"Waddup, lil' nigga? How shit looking out there?" he asked once Glock answered.

"Shit, my plan is unraveling. It's a little more complicated out here than the last mission, but it ain't nothing I can't handle," he assured confidently.

Murk nodded after adjusting the black White Sox baseball cap on his head. "I'm glad to hear that, but y'all got to head back this way... Big Body just got gunned down over on the westside, and Tory done lost his damn mind. He taking Big Body spot, and they on some renegade shit."

"I still got at least about thirty Glocks out there still.

That should be enough," Glock reasoned. "I got my momentum out here. Let me see this mission through."

"Nigga, that mission gone be pointless if the empire crumble out here. Rock Nation is ran off of its structure and discipline. Tory is threatening all of that. If the other cities catch wind that Rock Nation is losing its grip, then they'll start to plot and rebel like a muthafucka. BBG is a big threat, and we need all the soldiers we can get, just in case it's a real war, so get yo' lil' ass back up here. It's war time."

Glock sighed, but he agreed and ended the call.

"I'm not even gone lie, bruh. Even with us and the whole Glock Gang, that ain't near enough. BBG got all the numbers, and Tory know that shit. He gone hole himself up in them apartments and use it as a fortress 'cause he know we going to be gunning for his lil' bitch ass," Swiss calculated.

"I already know," Murk agreed with reluctance. "I'm gone get his ass though. Just let me brainstorm for a while. You know I'm gone find a way."

"Can't even take that from you. You *always* do," Swiss confirmed before accelerating a little faster as they headed down the expressway ramp.

———

Murk had fallen back asleep on the way to their destination. Swiss woke him up, letting him know they were there. Murk stretched deeply then looked around at the upper-class subdivision just outside the city. They were parked in front of a beautiful, three-story house that was probably in somebody's magazine somewhere. The house was immaculate. It didn't hold a candle to Laney's new castle, but it was definitely an elite piece of work.

The house belonged to Ice's family. His mother, father, sister, and brother stayed up under that roof. Ice didn't know Murk had the drop on that location, but he would soon find out.

"What, you want me to go to the door and bum-rush my way inside that muthafucka?" Swiss asked seriously.

Murk chuckled slightly. He was still kind of tired. He'd been up all night, playing *Call of Duty*. "Fuck no, nigga! That's home invasion, fool. We ain't got not one mask in this truck. Shit simple. Watch this."

He picked his iPhone up off of his lap and turned the video recorder on. "This your folks house, ain't it? Yeah, you see it, nigga. You got thirty fuckin' minutes to get here before I lose my patience," he spat before ending the recording and sending it to Ice's phone.

Seven minutes later, Ice was blowing up Murk's phone, but he didn't respond. He knew the feeling that Ice had in his stomach at the moment, and he wanted him to feel it. For all he knew, Murk could've been prepared to kill everything breathing in the house. Murk purposely powdered off his phone and was waiting for Ice.

"There he go!" Swiss spotted the AMG Benz and the Escalade truck right behind it. "Look like he brought some reinforcements," Swiss noted before reaching in the backseat to grab his HK SP5K.

Murk pocketed his phone and grabbed his AK-74. They both got out of the Range Rover and waited for them. They were parked on the curb of the house, but Ice and his company parked in the actual driveway of the house with the other cars.

Ice got out of his AMG alone, but four men hopped out of the Escalade, causing Murk to squint with his head sideways. "I know those movements too well."

"Yuuup! Them niggas got military background like a muthafucka," Swiss confirmed.

"What the fuck you got going on, Murk? Threatening my family and shit! I thought we was good with each other!" Ice spat once he was in hearing distance of them.

Swiss stood straight and firm, clutching his gun. Murk, on the other hand, leaned on the hood of the truck, completely unbothered. "We was good until you did that dumb ass shit. You don't even know what you done did, nigga. Tory done lost his muthafuckin' mind, and now he about to let BBG loose. They standing on their own now, and that's about to start a whole ass civil war. All because you want to get in the murder business."

Ice's face softened. "He left me no choice, Murk. You know that shit. The nigga kept pushing me. What else was I supposed to do?"

"Get the fuck out of dodge, like I told you. Now this nigga bringing war on all of our doorsteps because he can't confirm who did it."

Ice gave him a sideways look. "So, you didn't tell him it was me? Why?"

"Because you're going to get me a million dollars by the end of tomorrow. That's why," Murk informed matter-of-factly, daring Ice to oppose his offer.

Ice sighed dramatically. "Mannn, you killing me! I got

you though. I'll drop it off personally to your crib in the morning. You kept it real. I got to fuck with you."

"You right about that part," Murk agreed before pushing himself off of the truck's hood. "Oh, yeah, I know them the niggas you got to handle the business. They helped start this shit, and they ass going to help finish it. We need all the help we can get because y'all done woke up a fucking beast."

CHAPTER 44
GLOCK

"So, you're just going to abandon the whole mission? People out here on both sides of the field were looking forward to seeing what you were going to do. The Swamp Bullies have been terrorizing us for decades. If you was able to make that happen, you would've brought this town together," Kelsey envisioned verbally. She didn't even try to hide her disappointment.

"I'm not abandoning the mission. Trust me, I'll be back in no time, and I'm going to keep my word. I just have to go out there and show my face to make shit look good. Plus, I was going to have to go out there for my little sister's funeral anyway. Give me two weeks tops," he assured.

She sighed. "I hope you're being real with me right now."

Glock leaned on his car, that was parked in the very next parking spot to hers, and smiled at her. "If you gone miss a real nigga, just say that," he teased.

"Boy, shut up. Nobody's going to be thinking about you. I have better things to worry about."

"Like what? Your father's next sermon?" he joked.

She rolled her eyes. "Not funny!"

"Alright. That's my bad... But on some real shit, I done grew to fuck with you heavy, and I'm gone miss yo' lil' pretty ass. You helped me more than you know. Ain't even been thinking about my sister as much or nothin'," he admitted with much sincerity.

She stood there with wide eyes and an open mouth. "I can't believe it. You actually just showed me some kind of sensitivity... I'm glad I can do that for you. Now you need to hurry up and get back, so we can really get to know each other on another type of level. I like you, but I know you do bad things, so before I can deal with you in any type of way, I have to make sure there's a good man in there somewhere."

Glock didn't respond right away. He just licked his lips and took in her beauty. She was killing the sundress she wore, and Glock was determined to get up under that muthafucka. He knew her nectar was sweet as hell, and he wanted a permanent taste.

Before he could comeback with the smooth response he'd cooked up in his head, he noticed four modern pickup trucks riding throughout the complex. Two white men sat on the back of each truck, holding fully automatic rifles in hand. It was dark outside, but the apartment complex was well-lit due to all the streetlights.

The few soldiers that Glock had on lookout around the vicinity immediately got on their phones to call for reinforcements. They didn't know what type of time the crackers were on, so they prepared for whatever.

"What the fuck?!" Glock said to himself aloud.

"Oh, my God! Those are the Aryans!" Kelsey confirmed in a fearful tone. They didn't produce as much fear as the Swamp Bullies, but locals were definitely scared of them.

Glock wasn't though. "Go in my apartment. The first door to the left upstairs. Hurry up!" he commanded urgently before quickly opening up his car door to retrieve his brand-new M4 Carbine. Thanks to Murk, they had enough artillery to go to war with the National Guard.

Kelsey listened to him and rushed toward his building. He closed his door and joined two of his men that were standing at attention, waiting on the Aryans to make it to them. "They even blink too hard, light they pussy asses up!" Glock commanded firmly.

The trucks approached and came to a stop a few feet away from them. Well-built Aryans hopped out of the trucks dressed in camouflaged military gear. They moved like a militia for sure. Most of them had racist tattoos and bald heads. They were definitely Nazi descendants, if you asked Glock. The rest of Glock's calvary came from all different directions with guns in hand, ready for whatever. Glock was unfazed though. He stood his ground and waited for the racists to approach.

A tall, muscular man, that looked like he could be kin to the sheriff, came forward, leading the pack. He was the only one with hair on his head and casual clothes. He wore a grey Nike sweatsuit and a tennis cap to match. He looked

like an ordinary white man on the way to the gym or something. Glock knew better though.

"I'm here to see Glock," he informed as they neared.
"You're the only one with long braids, so I'm taking it
that's you." He visibly sized Glock up as the rest of his men
sized the Glockians up.

"Yeah, it's me. You must be Polar Bear... I can see why
they call you that," Glock said evenly. He surprised himself
by the lack of aggression he was displaying.

"I've been hearing that you're out here to try to take us
out. What's up with that, boy?"

Glock pursed his lips and nodded his head matter-of-
factly. "Yup. Right after I handle them Swamp niggas, I'm
on y'all ass, so get ready," he warned casually.

"Yeah, you must have a mental illness to really believe
that. I can see it in your eyes. There's not a doubt... You're
confident. I'll give you that."

"And I'm gone give you some advice. Make a deal with
me or die," he advised strongly with a straight face.

"And when he say die, he mean dead-dead. Like you
gone be washing Hitler's car windows, nigga," Ruga
chimed in, drawing laughter from the rest of the Glockians.

Polar Bear clenched his teeth. "If I didn't have so much
respect and history with the sheriff, I would make an
example out of you monkeys right now, but I'll just let the
Swamp Bullies handle my light work. You won't even
make it out of that swamp alive, so I'm not pressed... Good
luck, my niggers," he taunted disrespectfully before leading
the way back to their trucks.

"Aghhh! I wanna peel that nigga top back so bad!"
Ruga stressed, frustrated, as they were pulling off.

"Their day is coming real soon, bruh. Don't trip," Glock promised with all the confidence in the world. "Y'all niggas load up! We heading back to the city in the morning. Don't got to take everything though. We'll be back soon."

CHAPTER 45
ZION

Zion got word about Big Body and what Tory was doing all at the same time. His gym session wasn't over until 10:30 that night, and Lester had given him the whole rundown. He didn't even let Lester finish before he slipped his security and made his way over to Sandhurst solo.

His adrenaline was racing, his mind was racing, and most of all, his heart was hurting. Big Body was like a big brother to him, and he felt the loss deeply. He watched the news clip at a red light and had to cut it off. He couldn't even finish it. Once he saw Big Body's face on the screen, another wave of pain washed over him. It was real, but at the same time, it didn't feel real.

He was rolling into Sandhurst before he knew it. It was thick out there too. All types of people lounged around. Candles were burning here and there, barbeque grills were smoking, and music was playing. They were turning up for the biggest savage the westside had ever seen. Big Body was like a god on his side of town, and it showed. Everyone out there felt some type of pain from the loss of their big homie.

Zion cruised to the back of the complex and double parked by the park area. That was where all the action was, so that was where he needed to be. He hopped out of the dark grey GMC truck and made his way toward the basketball courts. There was a family-sized tent set up on the first court, and he knew that was exactly where he would find Tory.

He received mad love as he made his way to the tent — from the kids to the gangsters. It put a slight smirk on his face, but it disappeared quickly when two new faces stopped him at the entrance of the tent. "You can't go in there right now. They in a meeting."

"Go in there and tell Tory to come here, man," Zion said as politely as he could at the moment. This wasn't the time to be standing in his way of anything.

"Tory told us not to let *nobody* in," the other one stated defiantly, with his chest out, while gripping the big gun in his hand. He looked like a skinny version of Bernie Mac.

Zion sighed. "Everybody want to be hard," he noted before hitting the man with a crucial hook that sent him straight to the concrete floor with a broken jaw. He was out cold.

"Now what you want to bet I can break your whole face before you can get that gun pointed at me?" Zion challenged the other dude.

"Mannnn, I ain't fuckin' with you, Zion. Gone in there, man," the other dude decided wisely before making a show of stepping out of his way.

"Smart man," Zion said before proceeding into the tent.

All eyes were on him once he stepped into the tent. Tory and four other niggas sat around a plastic table that was set up in the main area of the tent. They were smoking and playing Poker. They looked surprised to see him.

"How the fuck you get in here, man?" Tory asked in an unpleasant tone. "Take your ass home, Zion. You made it out the streets. Stay out of this shit, bruh."

"You crashing out, bruh. I'm hurting about Body's death too, but you ain't got to do all this. You forcing Laney's hand. You ain't even give her a chance to handle the shit and make it right."

Tory grimaced and shook his head with disgust. "Nah, fuck that. They took my heart from me, bruh! I'm hurting, my nigga! The whole fuckin' world gone feel this shit. I'm gone make J-Rock look like a girl scout. Watch!"

"Listen... I see you clearly on one right now. You ain't in your right mind," Zion observed with his hands clasped together in prayer position. "All I'm going to tell you is that if you lay one finger on Laney, it's not gone be J-Rock or Murk you got to worry about. It's going to be me, nigga. She pregnant with my baby, nigga."

Tory shrugged. "Tell her to stay in a pregnant woman's place then! She ain't on my hit list, but if she get in my way, then I'm gone take her ass down. You just gone have to do what you got to do, and you know I ain't doing no fighting."

Zion stared at Tory with an intense death stare and clenched teeth. There was no need for him to respond any further. Everything that needed to be said had already been said, so he turned around and left.

———

About forty minutes later, Zion had finally made it back home. Laney was worried sick about him because he had his phone cut off while he was off the radar, and they got into a whole argument about it. But after that, he convinced her to hop in the inside hot tub with him, and he told her about the discussion he shared with Tory.

"That nigga hurting, bae, and I don't think he's going to come to his senses anytime soon. We going to have to put him down and restore balance out here. I see the tornado coming," he wisely advised.

She nodded her head. "Yeah, I know, but it ain't no *we*. Let me handle his ass. Murk going to take care of him."

"Listen here, woman. I don't care about that boxing shit, the money, or the fame, when it comes to you," he assured her with a straight face.

She just shook her head and slouched in the tub a little more. "Just let Murk do his job please. You're way too valuable to be involved, babe."

He closed the distance between them and held her in his arms. They were face to face, sharing an intense moment, when Laney's phone started vibrating on the edge of the tub. She hurriedly broke their embrace and rushed over to her phone, obviously hoping it was Murk with some good news, but her expression changed when she saw who it was calling.

She answered the phone and put it on speaker. "What you want, J-Rock?"

"Why the fuck I got to hear about all this shit from

other folks? You supposed to let me know about some shit like that. I specifically told you to let me know about any extreme emergencies," J-Rock barked into the phone with his usual aggressiveness.

Laney's face crumbled up like she'd just swallowed some very spoiled milk. "Man, what the fuck you mean?! Call you for what, nigga? What you supposed to do all the way from Jamaica? You gave me a job, and I'm trying my best to do it! Tory will be dead sooner than later... Go sip on some coconut juice or something."

Zion's anxiety spiked, hearing his woman talk to J-Rock like that. He was easily one of the most dangerous men on the East Coast. He caught himself silently praying J-Rock didn't take her disrespect too harshly.

"Nah, that lil' nigga is mines!" J-Rock informed firmly. "I got to kill him myself. I'll be out there in a few days."

"Now you talking, nigga!" she spat with much relief in her tone. "You want me to tell Murk to chill then?"

"Yeah, everybody need to sit the fuck down until I get there! We'll sit at the round table when I do," he informed then instructed.

"You need to bring some reinforcements because we're shorthanded like a muthafucka. Tory got a whole ass army behind him. You know how deep BBG is... They done got even bigger," she reminded seriously.

J-Rock didn't respond right away. "Alright, say no more. I'll bring some dread heads with me," he assured before ending the call.

"I got to have a talk with J-Rock — face to face, man to man — when he come back. Got to get you out of that lifestyle... I can't stand to see you worry like this," Zion admitted sincerely.

She shifted back into his arms. "It's going to work out, baby. I got something up my sleeve. Watch. I'll be a whole ass stay at home mom before this baby is here," she promised confidently.

TO BE CONTINUED....

LOCK DOWN PUBLICATIONS AND CA$H PRESENTS

ASSISTED PUBLISHING PACKAGES

BASIC PACKAGE	UPGRADED PACKAGE
$499	$800
Editing	Typing
Cover Design	Editing
Formatting	Cover Design
	Formatting

ADVANCE PACKAGE	LDP SUPREME PACKAGE
$1,200	$1,500
Typing	Typing
Editing	Editing
Cover Design	Cover Design
Formatting	Formatting
Copyright registration	Copyright registration
Proofreading	Proofreading
Upload book to Amazon	Set up Amazon account
	Upload book to Amazon
	Advertise on LDP, Amazon and Facebook Page

NEW RELEASES

BLOODLINE OF A SAVAGE 1&2
THESE VICIOUS STREETS 1&2
RELENTLESS GOON
RELENTLESS GOON 2
BY PRINCE A. TAUHID

THE BUTTERFLY MAFIA 1-3
BY FUMIYA PAYNE

A THUG'S STREET PRINCESS 1&2
BY MEESHA

CITY OF SMOKE 2
BY MOLOTTI

STEPPERS 1,2&3
THE REAL BADDIES OF CHI-RAQ
BY KING RIO

THE LANE 1&2
BY KEN-KEN SPENCE

THUG OF SPADES 1&2
LOVE IN THE TRENCHES 2
CORNER BOYS
BY COREY ROBINSON

TIL DEATH 3

BY ARYANNA

THE BIRTH OF A GANGSTER 4
BY DELMONT PLAYER

PRODUCT OF THE STREETS 1&2
BY DEMOND "MONEY" ANDERSON

NO TIME FOR ERROR
BY KEESE

MONEY HUNGRY DEMONS
BY TRANAY ADAMS

Coming Soon from Lock Down Publications/Ca$h Presents

IF YOU CROSS ME ONCE 6
ANGEL V
By Anthony Fields

IMMA DIE BOUT MINE 5
By Aryanna

A THUGS STREET PRINCESS 3
By Meesha

PRODUCT OF THE STREETS 3
By Demond Money Anderson

CORNER BOYS 2
By Corey Robinson

THE MURDER QUEENS 6&7
By Michael Gallon

CITY OF SMOKE 3
By Molotti

CONFESSIONS OF A DOPE BOY
By Nicholas Lock

THA TAKEOVER
By Keith Chandler

Coming Soon

BETRAYAL OF A G 2
By Ray Vinci

CRIME BOSS
By Playa Ray

Available Now

RESTRAINING ORDER 1 & 2
By CA$H & Coffee

LOVE KNOWS NO BOUNDARIES 1-3
By Coffee

RAISED AS A GOON I, II, III & IV
BRED BY THE SLUMS I, II, III
BLAST FOR ME I & II
ROTTEN TO THE CORE I II III
A BRONX TALE I, II, III
DUFFLE BAG CARTEL I II III IV V VI
HEARTLESS GOON I II III IV V
A SAVAGE DOPEBOY I II
DRUG LORDS I II III
CUTTHROAT MAFIA I II
KING OF THE TRENCHES
By Ghost

LAY IT DOWN I & II
LAST OF A DYING BREED I II
BLOOD STAINS OF A SHOTTA I & II III
By Jamaica

Coming Soon

LOYAL TO THE GAME I II III
LIFE OF SIN I, II III
By TJ & Jelissa

IF LOVING HIM IS WRONG…I & II
LOVE ME EVEN WHEN IT HURTS I II III
By Jelissa

PUSH IT TO THE LIMIT
By Bre' Hayes

BLOODY COMMAS I & II
SKI MASK CARTEL I, II & III
KING OF NEW YORK I II, III IV V
RISE TO POWER I II III
COKE KINGS I II III IV V
BORN HEARTLESS I II III IV
KING OF THE TRAP I II
By T.J. Edwards

WHEN THE STREETS CLAP BACK I & II III
THE HEART OF A SAVAGE I II III IV
MONEY MAFIA I II
LOYAL TO THE SOIL I II III
By Jibril Williams

A DISTINGUISHED THUG STOLE MY HEART I
II & III
LOVE SHOULDN'T HURT I II III IV
RENEGADE BOYS 1-4
PAID IN KARMA 1-3

Coming Soon

SAVAGE STORMS 1-3
AN UNFORESEEN LOVE 1-3
BABY, I'M WINTERTIME COLD 1-3
A THUG'S STREET PRINCESS 1&2
By Meesha

A GANGSTER'S CODE 1-3
A GANGSTER'S SYN 1-3
THE SAVAGE LIFE 1-3
CHAINED TO THE STREETS 1-3
BLOOD ON THE MONEY 1-3
A GANGSTA'S PAIN 1-3
BEAUTIFUL LIES AND UGLY TRUTHS
CHURCH IN THESE STREETS
By J-Blunt

CUM FOR ME 1-8
An LDP Erotica Collaboration

BLOOD OF A BOSS 1-5
SHADOWS OF THE GAME
TRAP BASTARD
By Askari

THE STREETS BLEED MURDER 1-3
THE HEART OF A GANGSTA 1-3
By Jerry Jackson

WHEN A GOOD GIRL GOES BAD
By Adrienne

THE COST OF LOYALTY 1-3
By Kweli

BRIDE OF A HUSTLA 1-3
THE FETTI GIRLS 1-3
CORRUPTED BY A GANGSTA 1-4
BLINDED BY HIS LOVE
THE PRICE YOU PAY FOR LOVE 1-3
DOPE GIRL MAGIC 1-3
By Destiny Skai

A KINGPIN'S AMBITION
A KINGPIN'S AMBITION II
I MURDER FOR THE DOUGH
By Ambitious

TRUE SAVAGE 1-7
DOPE BOY MAGIC 1-3
MIDNIGHT CARTEL 1-3
CITY OF KINGZ 1&2
NIGHTMARE ON SILENT AVE
THE PLUG OF LIL MEXICO 1&2
CLASSIC CITY
By Chris Green

A GANGSTER'S REVENGE 1-4
THE BOSS MAN'S DAUGHTERS 1-5
A SAVAGE LOVE 1&2
BAE BELONGS TO ME 1&2
A HUSTLER'S DECEIT 1-3
WHAT BAD BITCHES DO 1-3

STREET KINGS 1&2
PAID IN BLOOD 1&2
CARTEL KILLAZ 1-3
DOPE GODS 1&2
By Hood Rich

THE STREETS ARE CALLING
By Duquie Wilson

STEADY MOBBN' 1-3
THE STREETS STAINED MY SOUL 1-3
By Marcellus Allen

WHO SHOT YA 1-3
SON OF A DOPE FIEND 1-4
HEAVEN GOT A GHETTO 1&2
SKI MASK MONEY 1&2
By Renta

GORILLAZ IN THE BAY 1-4
TEARS OF A GANGSTA 1/&2
3X KRAZY 1&2
STRAIGHT BEAST MODE 1&2
By DE'KARI

TRIGGADALE 1-3
MURDA WAS THE CASE 1-3
By Elijah R. Freeman

SLAUGHTER GANG 1-3
RUTHLESS HEART 1-3

Coming Soon

By Willie Slaughter

GOD BLESS THE TRAPPERS 1-3
THESE SCANDALOUS STREETS 1-3
FEAR MY GANGSTA 1-5
THESE STREETS DON'T LOVE NOBODY 1-2
BURY ME A G 1-5
A GANGSTA'S EMPIRE 1-4
THE DOPEMAN'S BODYGAURD 1&2
THE REALEST KILLAZ 1-3
THE LAST OF THE OGS 1-3
By Tranay Adams

MARRIED TO A BOSS 1-3
By Destiny Skai & Chris Green

KINGZ OF THE GAME 1-7
CRIME BOSS 1-3
By Playa Ray

FUK SHYT
By Blakk Diamond

DON'T F#CK WITH MY HEART 1&2
By Linnea

ADDICTED TO THE DRAMA 1-3
IN THE ARM OF HIS BOSS
By Jamila

LOYALTY AIN'T PROMISED 1&2

Coming Soon

By Keith Williams

YAYO 1-4
A SHOOTER'S AMBITION 1&2
BRED IN THE GAME
By S. Allen

TRAP GOD 1-3
RICH $AVAGE 1-3
MONEY IN THE GRAVE 1-3
CARTEL MONEY
By Martell Troublesome Bolden

FOREVER GANGSTA 1&2
GLOCKS ON SATIN SHEETS 1&2
By Adrian Dulan

TOE TAGZ 1-4
LEVELS TO THIS SHYT 1&2
IT'S JUST ME AND YOU
By Ah'Million

KINGPIN DREAMS 1-3
RAN OFF ON DA PLUG
By Paper Boi Rari

THE STREETS MADE ME 1-3
By Larry D. Wright

CONFESSIONS OF A GANGSTA 1-4
CONFESSIONS OF A JACKBOY 1-3

Coming Soon

CONFESSIONS OF A HITMAN
By Nicholas Lock

I'M NOTHING WITHOUT HIS LOVE
SINS OF A THUG
TO THE THUG I LOVED BEFORE
A GANGSTA SAVED XMAS
IN A HUSTLER I TRUST
By Monet Dragun

QUIET MONEY 1-3
THUG LIFE 1-3
EXTENDED CLIP 1&2
A GANGSTA'S PARADISE
By Trai'Quan

CAUGHT UP IN THE LIFE 1-3
THE STREETS NEVER LET GO 1-3
By Robert Baptiste

NEW TO THE GAME 1-3
MONEY, MURDER & MEMORIES 1-3
By Malik D. Rice

CREAM 2-3
THE STREETS WILL TALK
By Yolanda Moore

THE STREETS WILL NEVER CLOSE 1-3
By K'ajji

LIFE OF A SAVAGE 1-4
A GANGSTA'S QUR'AN 1-4
MURDA SEASON 1-3
GANGLAND CARTEL 1-3
CHI'RAQ GANGSTAS 1-4
KILLERS ON ELM STREET 1-3
JACK BOYZ N DA BRONX 1-3
A DOPEBOY'S DREAM 1-3
JACK BOYS VS DOPE BOYS 1-3
COKE GIRLZ
COKE BOYS
SOSA GANG 1&2
BRONX SAVAGES
BODYMORE KINGPINS
BLOOD OF A GOON
By Romell Tukes

CONCRETE KILLA 1-3
VICIOUS LOYALTY 1-3
By Kingpen

THE ULTIMATE SACRIFICE 1-6
KHADIFI
IF YOU CROSS ME ONCE 1-3
ANGEL 1-4
IN THE BLINK OF AN EYE
By Anthony Fields

THE LIFE OF A HOOD STAR
By Ca$h & Rashia Wilson

Coming Soon

STEPPERS 1-3
SUPER GREMLIN 1-4
By King Rio

MONEY GAME 1&2
By Smoove Dolla

A GANGSTA'S KARMA 1-4
By FLAME

KING OF THE TRENCHES 1-3
By GHOST & TRANAY ADAMS

QUEEN OF THE ZOO 1&2
By Black Migo

GRIMEY WAYS 1-3
BETRAYAL OF A G
By Ray Vinci

XMAS WITH AN ATL SHOOTER
By Ca$h & Destiny Skai

KING KILLA 1&2
By Vincent "Vitto" Holloway

BETRAYAL OF A THUG 1&2
By Fre$h

THE MURDER QUEENS 1-5
By Michael Gallon

FOR THE LOVE OF BLOOD 1-4
By Jamel Mitchell

HOOD CONSIGLIERE 1&2
NO TIME FOR ERROR
By Keese

PROTÉGÉ OF A LEGEND 1&2
LOVE IN THE TRENCHES 1&2
By Corey Robinson

THE PLUG'S RUTHLESS DAUGHTER
By Tony Daniels

BORN IN THE GRAVE 1-3
CRIME PAYS
By Self Made Tay

MOAN IN MY MOUTH
By XTASY

TORN BETWEEN A GANGSTER AND A
GENTLEMAN
By J-BLUNT & Miss Kim

LOYALTY IS EVERYTHING 1-3
CITY OF SMOKE 1&2
By Molotti

HERE TODAY GONE TOMORROW 1&2
By Fly Rock

BOOKS BY LDP'S CEO, CA$H

TRUST IN NO MAN

TRUST IN NO MAN 2

TRUST IN NO MAN 3

BONDED BY BLOOD

SHORTY GOT A THUG

THUGS CRY

THUGS CRY 2

THUGS CRY 3

TRUST NO BITCH

TRUST NO BITCH 2

TRUST NO BITCH 3

TIL MY CASKET DROPS

RESTRAINING ORDER

RESTRAINING ORDER 2

IN LOVE WITH A CONVICT

LIFE OF A HOOD STAR

XMAS WITH AN ATL SHOOTER

www.ingramcontent.com/pod-product-compliance
Lightning Source LLC
Chambersburg PA
CBHW070457260626
47161CB00004B/1336

* 9 7 8 1 9 6 5 4 4 8 0 8 3 *